SUGAR-COATED KISSES

SUGARED AND SPICED
BOOK THREE

LADY MARIE

Cover design by Lady Marie

Editing by A.K. Edits

Formatting by Author Mya

CONTENTS

For anyone who's ever been afraid to step out of their comfort zone.

CONTENT WARNING

This book features explicit sexual content, discussions of mutually beneficial sugar arrangements, and briefly mentions the death of a spouse due to drunk driving.

Read with care and have fun!

CHAPTER ONE
ARTHUR

THE DULL POUNDING IN MY HEAD WOULDN'T GO away, no matter how hard I tried.

To be fair, that "try hard" attempt was really just me taking two ibuprofen within thirty minutes of getting to the Sugared and Spiced clubhouse and chasing them with two fingers of scotch. Was that the best idea? Probably not, but it was the only sure-fire way I was going to get through the night.

"How did I let them talk me into this?"

"You know, I wouldn't necessarily say talking to yourself is a cause for concern." My best friend's voice filled the space next to me, drowning out everyone else in the room. "But when you're doing it in a place like this, full of beautiful ass people, at least half of whom are staring at you like they want you to take a bite out of them, I've got to admit it worries me," he snickered.

I cut my eyes over at Seth as he leaned against the bar, looking perfectly at home as he ordered a drink of his own. In a way, I guess he was since this was his scene a lot more than mine. After all, he was the actual Sugared and Spiced member. The way he seemed so at ease made me feel more than a little jealous and set my nerves on edge even more. "Don't start."

"What?" he asked, feigning innocence, though the glint in his eye and smirk playing on his lips told me he knew exactly what I was referring to.

"Fine. Since you don't want me talking to myself, I'll just ask you. How the hell did I let you talk me into coming to this damn thing?"

"Awww, come on, Artie, you say that like this is some big, scary monster. It's just a small, private party filled with people who want to get to know each other. People who want to get to know *you*. Take it from me when I say this is a guaranteed good time." One of the bartenders sat what looked like a bourbon on the rocks in front of him, and he quickly grabbed it to take a sip. "Besides, you didn't let *me* do anything. You let *her* do it." Seth tilted his head across the room, the movement perfectly matched with the moment his wife appeared.

The asshole had me there. Seth trying to convince me to attend the Sugared and Spiced masquerade night hadn't had any effect. In fact, turning down his initial invitation had been easy. I'd just explained that my time was already occupied, but I appreciated the thought. Of course, that led to a string of questions about what my mysterious plans actually were. I'd made up one thing or another because while my mysterious plans might not exist, I was content finding something else to do with my time that didn't involve my friends attempting to set me up through their beloved sugar baby website. No offense to them, but despite Seth, Melinda, and our friend Benjamin, who was also hanging around here somewhere, being active members, it just wasn't my bottle of scotch *or* cup of tea.

In true Seth fashion, he'd refused to give up, asking me multiple times for the next three weeks and getting the same response every time. When I noticed his car pulling into my driveway five days ago, I'd been prepped and ready to repeat myself one final time—only it wasn't him paying me a visit. It was Melinda. God help me, that woman had always been impossible to say no to. I couldn't think of anyone who might be immune to her powers, least of all Seth and the gorgeous brunette turned redhead, Alaina, who'd just entered the room right behind her.

"You know as well as I do that when Mel has her mind set on something, nothing and no one can get her to change it. Well...except maybe Alaina."

As much as I wanted to grumble, I didn't. Seth was right, though I wasn't going to give him the satisfaction of admitting it.

Apparently, he didn't need me to, taking just a few seconds to throw back the rest of his drink before stepping away to meet the two women who were already headed in our direction. He placed a loving kiss on both of their lips, starting with the wife that I'd been friends with for years and then moving to the girlfriend they shared, who I was quickly coming to know and love as well. The trio had become practically inseparable since meeting last year. It was sweet how they all doted on one another. So sweet that it was hard to ignore the pang I felt whenever I was in their presence.

Melinda managed to pry herself away from her better halves and sidle up alongside me. "I hope Seth isn't giving you a hard time, Arthur. I told him to be on his best behavior tonight." She pulled me in for a hug and gave me a once-over.

"We both know that is a rare and difficult task for him." I chuckled.

"Very true, Artie, but Seth is supposed to have some extra incentive to follow directions tonight." Alaina appeared next to her and gave me a quick kiss on the cheek before wrapping her arms around her date's waist. "If he can't behave himself, then he won't be able to join in on the fun."

"Is that so?" I smirked, turning my gaze toward the troublemaker himself.

"Mhmm. I don't know if you've figured this out yet, but while Seth here might love to watch, it's torture for him when he can't touch. Isn't that right, Daddy?"

I could feel my ears heating at Alaina's words as she batted her eyelashes up at him. The only thing I could do was take what she said in stride. At this point, knowing my best friends' dirty little not-so-secrets was par for the course. He shot her a wink and a smile.

"Well then, I guess you better be nice to me, *Daddy*. Wouldn't want you to miss out."

"Don't call me that," he grumbled, though there was no real agitation to my old friend's words. "And I don't think I like the fact that you're all ganging up on me right now. Especially since I'm not giving him a hard time at all. Arthur's doing a great job of that on his own. I was just doing my due diligence and making sure he was ready for the fun he's about to have."

"Mmm, I don't know if I believe you," said Melinda.

"You wound me, angel." Snatching Alaina away from her, I could just make out him whispering, "I bet our girl here believes me."

His hand began to inch down past her exposed stomach and her eyes fluttered closed. I quickly averted my gaze, not needing to catch a glimpse of whatever *that* was leading to.

"There's really no reason for you to be nervous, Arthur." As her partners occupied themselves, Melinda slipped her arm under mine, completely unfazed.

"Nervous isn't exactly how I'd put it," I said sheepishly, though that was probably the best descriptor for what I was feeling.

"I told you, nothing happens here that you don't want to. No promises and no commitments."

I snorted, considering being afraid of commitment had never been my problem.

"Tonight is about having fun, releasing your inhibitions, and discovering something new about yourself." Melinda smiled, slipping away and giving me a bit of space. "That's what this is for, remember?" She held up the simple forest green mask I'd placed on the bar and took it upon herself to secure it on my face, careful to push my long locs out of the way.

"And they already did the hard part of finding a date for you."

A smiling Benji appeared, Sage right by his side, and

clapped me on the shoulder. What was this, Gang Up on Arthur Night? I seriously hoped the five of them didn't intend to spend the night babysitting me because that was going to get old very quickly. At forty-six years old, I was more than capable of looking out for myself, even if this was an unfamiliar situation.

An exasperated sigh left me before I could stop it. "Is that supposed to make me feel better?"

"Oh, come on, Arthur. You're telling me all those messages I saw between you two yesterday don't have you the least bit excited about meeting this woman in person?"

Of course Benji would bring that up. The one pitfall of spending so much time with my best friends was that none of them had any problem invading my privacy. You'd think they'd have their hands full with their own business, but somehow, they still found time for mine too.

After finally getting me agree to participate in the masquerade festivities, Melinda let me in on all the important details, including the fact that me being currently unattached gave me the option of being matched with a date for the night via an online survey similar to the one members completed when they signed up for Sugared and Spiced or going in and letting my match come naturally during the night.

My first instinct was to decline the matchmaking—just the thought was enough for me to try and change my mind about participating at all—but once again, Melinda refused to take no for an answer. She even went as far as to offer up her services to complete the thing with me.

Yeah, no. I might have been privy to my friends' quirks and kinks, but that didn't mean I wanted them to know mine. Once I assured her that wasn't necessary and promised to follow through with the form, Melinda left me to my own devices.

In all honesty, I hadn't taken the questionnaire seriously, though I made sure to answer honestly. Just because I had low expectations for the night didn't mean I was suddenly going to become a liar and potentially ruin someone else's good time. At least I hadn't been forced to share my real name with anyone beyond the administrators. For safety purposes, everyone had to submit a valid government-issued ID, but to ensure the air of mystery was upheld, a little note at the bottom of the page promised that only a nickname of my choosing and brief description of my appearance would be shared with my match.

After hitting *submit*, I carried on with the rest of my day, not giving it any more thought. At least not until the next day when an email arrived with a simple greeting, instructions on how to download the secure messaging app, and a name: Trini. Even after placing the app on my phone, since it also held my unique QR code to gain entry to the event, I had every intention of writing it off and resolving myself to just meeting her tonight, no precursor necessary. Then the first message appeared on my screen.

One message turned into two, two into three. Even now, just the thought of them had me intrigued about who could have possibly been on the other side of the screen and what it would be like when we met. It was clear we were both a bit apprehensive about the whole thing, but that was enough to make me not regret agreeing to participate. I could only hope since Trini assured me she would still be coming tonight that the same could be said for her. Now that I was actually here, though, my confidence was waning just a bit.

And so there I stood, a second drink in hand, testing the three-drink limit, wondering one more time as my eyes scanned the room, *what the fuck have I gotten myself into?*

A TEXT INTERLUDE

TRINI:

So…it looks like we're a match

I have to be honest though, I don't
really understand what that means.

ARJAY:

> I don't really know what it means
> either, but hi. It's nice to meet you…so
> to speak.

TRINI:

Oh shit, I forgot to say that, didn't I?
Sorry. I guess I'm kind of nervous.

Actually, scratch that. I'm very
nervous.

That and my best friend is currently
watching me like a hawk to make sure
I'm actually messaging you

ARJAY:

Trust me, you're not the only one. With nerves I mean. I managed to get my best friend to let me do this part alone.

TRINI:

That's...actually reassuring

Does that mean you're not a S&S member?

ARJAY:

Definitely not. I don't even think I do that great a job at regular flirting so something like this is out of my wheelhouse.

I'm more S&S adjacent. Most of my friends are members and somehow, they've roped me into giving this a try.

At least for one night anyway. How about you?

TRINI:

Lucky for me then? At least I hope so.

I don't know if I've been in Oakwood long enough to even be a member

But my best friend wanted to try this out and she always manages to get me to tag along so....here we are

ARJAY:

Here we are

TRINI:

I have to ask, did your parents
actually name you Arjay thinking it
was cute or is this a play on your
initials, RJ?

ARJAY:

Lol, neither. More like a nickname I
picked up in college that no one calls
me anymore.

It's a mashup of my first and middle
names

TRINI:

Interesting

ARJAY:

I think so. How did you come up with
Trini?

TRINI:

I'd tell you, but then I might have to
hurt you

ARJAY:

And we wouldn't want that, now
would we?

TRINI:

Idk. It might be something you're into.

TRINI:

Guess I'll find out soon enough, right?

ARJAY:

Guess you will...

CHAPTER TWO

TRINITY

"I don't know why you can't trust me when I say tonight is just what you need in your life."

"Because the last time you said that to me, I ended up having to call my mama at three-thirty in the morning to help bail you out of jail," I deadpanned, shooting my best friend Khrys a look that screamed 'be fucking for real' as the car pulled up to a very nondescript, slightly sketchy warehouse.

"Trinity, it's very much time for you to let that go. It's been like seven years at this point. We've grown."

"More like two and a half years, and considering how you cussed that rideshare driver out two nights ago, it's safe to say you haven't grown that much." I giggled since this time it was Khrys shooting me the death stare. "I'm just kidding!"

Sort of. She really had cussed out our rideshare driver as we were coming home from happy hour, and even though the creep deserved it for the very racist things he'd been saying to us, I was sure he was going to call the police.

Not wasting any more time, we climbed out of our current rideshare, which I'm sure the woman was happy about since we hadn't shut up since she picked us up thirty minutes ago. Part of me wanted to get right back in and have her take me back to Khrys's apartment, but I resisted the urge and instead followed my bestie to the front of what was supposedly the exclusive Sugared and Spiced clubhouse, marked by the *S&S* scrolled across the black door in gold calligraphy.

"Like I was saying before you tried to get cute," Khrys said, leading the way, "this masquerade party is the best place for you to unwind. No one here knows who you are and vice versa. It's the perfect excuse to let loose and get a little wild. And from what I've heard, there's something on the menu for everyone. You and your lil' cookie have gone way too long without some good, nasty fun. As *thee* most decorated best friend in the entire world, I'm here to tell you that you've moved past sad and you're very close to entering pathetic territory."

Well, damn. As much as I wanted to cuss her out for that little remark, she wasn't lying. To anyone else, it may have sounded like a bit much, but I knew better than anyone that Khrys always spoke her mind and didn't sugarcoat things. My sex and love lives—or lack thereof, at this point—really had become pathetic.

At twenty-six, I wasn't a virgin, but I also wasn't all that experienced either. My "lil' cookie," as Khrys put it, had stayed right in the jar until I was twenty-one. A few times was more than enough to know that sex with that particular person left a lot to be desired. About a year after that, I ended up falling for my ex-boyfriend, Kalvin, who was, coincidentally, Khrys's twin brother. After just over three years together in what I thought was a happy relationship headed for marriage, he finally let me know that he couldn't deal with our "lackluster" sex life anymore. Or at least that was the excuse he gave for cheating on me for half of our relationship. Because she absolutely loved me more than his trifling ass, Khrys had dragged him from top to bottom when she found out and put the cherry lollipop on top by breaking his nose, too.

Kalvin was nothing if not a cliché, and while he was full of shit for putting the blame on me and my inexperience for why he cheated, he wasn't wrong about our sex life. Hell, most days even playing with myself ended in disappointment. If making myself come was a chore more often than not, how could I expect anyone else to have the patience to try and get the job done? So yeah, attending an event hosted by the premier sugar baby and matchmaking company in Oakwood wasn't exactly filling me with excitement.

But instead of saying all that as we walked through the threshold and up to the host stand where a very fine ass man was standing, I shot back, "Just because you stay hot and ready like a Lil' Caesars pizza doesn't mean I have to."

"First of all," Khrys said, eyes narrowed, "don't ever in your life compare this Michelin star meal between my thighs to a nasty ass Lil' Caesars pizza again. How dare you?"

I couldn't help but giggle at her foolishness.

Getting stuck with a best friend who was a hot ass mess had not been the original plan during freshman year of college, but Student Housing had other ideas. She'd been fighting to get me out of my shell for the last eight years, and it worked most days. Even now, when we lived in two different cities, Khrys still made a point to call me to make sure I wasn't just rotting away at home doing the same thing day in and day out. With me thinking about moving to Oakwood, I knew I'd need to get myself ready to take more of these little excursions with her. They may not all be Sugared and Spiced-coded, but there was no doubt in my mind that they'd all be interesting.

"I'm just saying this isn't what I came to Oakwood for." My voice sounded whiny, even to my own ears, but I couldn't help it.

"No, you came to Oakwood to spend time with a dad you didn't even know existed. Going out with me tonight to find yourself a daddy, that's an added bonus."

Oh, this girl really was on one, huh? I didn't even get to respond because she held up her hand to cut me off, then directed her attention to the man in front of us. Irritating ass.

"Entry for two, please," she said, batting her eyelashes and raising her phone for him to scan. I followed suit, though he barely paid me any attention, too busy focusing on her. After checking the scanner to make sure our QR codes came up as authentic, he gestured toward a small table to his right.

"Ladies, please choose a mask and follow me."

Nerves hit me again all at once. "Khrys, I don't know. All of this is way out of my league. Why does it feel like we were just given permission to see the Holy Grail?"

"The Holy Grail doesn't have shit on this," she laughed while searching the table. "It's not easy to get a golden ticket to one of these things. Especially since they're usually reserved for members only."

"Then how did you manage it?" There was no way she was a member. I would've heard about it long before now. Khrys never could hold water, especially when it came to something this juicy.

When I got the email letting me know that I was invited as Khrys Colson's plus-one, followed by the instructions on what I needed to do if I planned on participating, confusion wasn't even the word. And of course, she was no help. When I called to ask what the hell she'd signed me up for, her only response was that I didn't have a choice and not to be a pain in her ass. No explanation, no information. Everything I knew about Sugared and Spiced came solely from the email and web search I'd done, and even that didn't turn up a whole lot of information. Secrecy was clearly part of the brand.

"Let's just say a friend of a friend helped me out." Her fingers scooped up a barely-there lace mask that matched her sheer lace red dress. Both left little to the imagination, like she was begging someone to recognize her.

"Khrys, stop playing with me! I will go home right now."

"Oh, come on, you're really going to come all this

way just to turn around? What about your mystery date? Didn't you promise him you'd meet him tonight?"

Okay, she had me there, but enough was enough. Khrys was going to have to give me something other than vague answers if she really wanted me to go through with this. I might have waited 'til the last minute to put my foot down, but so what? It was not too late for me to take my Black ass right on home.

"He'll be fine. All we did was send each other a few text messages. It's not that serious." More like several text messages over the last few days, but she didn't need to know that. "I'm so serious right now, Khrys. You better tell me something!"

"Okay, okay," she finally caved with an exasperated sigh. "The S&S PR team wanted to revamp their website and one of their members put me on their radar. I did a boudoir shoot for this girl and she asked if I was taking on any new graphic design clients. Actually...she might be here tonight."

"One of your clients is a member? That was your connect?"

Slipping her mask over her braids, Khrys nodded. "S&S is how she met the married couple she's dating. The shoot was actually her Valentine's Day gift to them. Very sexy. Some of my best work, if I do say so myself."

"A married couple?!" Did she think we were just going to gloss over that little tidbit? Yeah, no.

"Told you there's something here for everyone. And trust me when I say they treat her very, very well." She shot me a wink and made sure her mask was in place.

"Now hurry up and pick a mask. You have a secret admirer waiting for you, and I have a few."

I really needed to reevaluate my friends after this was over.

Nibbling on my bottom lip, I looked over the table before finally reaching for a simple black mask. It reminded me of the sort of thing an old-school superhero might wear to conceal their identity—plain, but it would get the job done. I smirked at the thought because it was the exact style I'd mentioned to Arjay in one of our messages. Khrys would kill me if she knew that I'd let my nerdy side show, but he didn't seem to mind.

Just as I resolved myself to head into the main room, something caught my eye. A few inches away from the mask I'd picked up was one that was the complete opposite. Made up of what looked like iridescent jewels, it caught the dim lighting in the entryway, sending sparkles and rainbows across the space at random.

What if I—

No. I turned, shaking the thought out of my head because the damn thing didn't even match my black mini dress and it definitely wasn't what Arjay would be looking for. Still, for some reason, even as I took a step away from the table, I couldn't get the beautiful jewels out of my mind.

"Triniiiii!"

Before I could second-guess myself—and before Khrys's head started to spin around and fly off—I switched the mask in my hand for the jeweled accessory that had me in a chokehold. Maybe I wasn't one hundred percent convinced that this was where I should be spending my Saturday night. Maybe this was a big ass mistake and I'd regret every minute of it.

Or maybe my best friend was right and this was exactly what I needed right now. If it was the third option, I guess that meant I wouldn't trade her in just yet. The jury might be out on that last one, but either way, I wouldn't know if I didn't try.

A TEXT INTERLUDE

ARJAY:

I can't tell you the last time I wore a mask, but I'm sure it's been at least a decade

TRINI:

Would you believe me if I said it's only been eight months for me?

ARJAY:

I'm inclined to both believe you and ask you what was the occasion

TRINI:

What do you mean? It was just a regular Friday night.

ARJAY:

...

TRINI:

Just kidding. Halloween. I was Catwoman…sort of.

ARJAY:

The Halle Berry version or Michelle Pfeiffer?

Either way, I have to say I approve

TRINI:

Look at you dropping a few pop culture references. I'm impressed.

ARJAY:

Don't be. I might have streamed a few movies after you mentioned your slight obsession with all things comic and superhero related yesterday.

TRINI:

I don't think Catwoman technically qualifies as a superhero, but effort noted

ARJAY:

Well, you did mention she's your favorite, didn't you?

TRINI:

I did...touché

ARJAY:

So...

Are you going to answer my question? Halle or Michelle?

TRINI:

Sorry to say, neither. Is there such a thing as a sweet cat burglar? Because that's a bit more on brand for me.

ARJAY:

A sweet cat burglar huh? Sounds a lot better than both Halle and Michelle in my opinion.

TRINI:

You are so full of it 🙄

ARJAY:

I'm going to assume you mean that in the best way possible 🙃

TRINI:

Assume away lol

You might just be right

ARJAY:

Oh I know I am. I have a sixth sense about these things.

Which is how I know I'm absolutely right about the sweet cat burglar appeal. Don't worry. You can prove me right this Saturday.

TRINI:

By wearing the same one?

ARJAY:

I'm sure they'll have a simple black mask in your size

TRINI:

Like you could really be that lucky

ARJAY:

Something tells me I just might be

CHAPTER THREE
ARTHUR

I was thirty seconds away from leaving and calling it a night. After having to endure forty-five minutes of suggestive smirks, arm caresses, and more introductions than any one person should ever be subjected to, and Trini nowhere in sight, I was ready to slip out, disappear into my car, and make my way home.

Home is exactly where you belong because this is not for you. But you already knew that.

That annoying little voice wasn't wrong. The idea of Sugared and Spiced didn't offend me in any way. How could it when three of my four best friends were currently members and had found their significant others using their services? Even the concept of sugar babies wasn't new to me. I was well aware of how Seth and Alaina had originally met, and whether society wanted to admit it or not, this sort of thing had been around since the beginning of time.

Despite all of those things, I'd never pictured myself in this sort of situation. By definition, I was pretty traditional when it came to relationships. The wife with two point five kids and a white picket fence were all part of the future I'd wanted to carve out for myself for as long as I could remember. In fact, I'd been well on my way to having it all, but turned out it wasn't exactly in the cards for me.

Laura was the love of my life. Meeting her at nineteen turned my world upside down in ways I could never have imagined. Ways I couldn't have prepared for. We'd fallen head over heels in love from the moment we set eyes on each other, and when we decided to elope just six months later, there was no doubt in my mind that it was the best decision I'd ever make. For ten years, she was the light of my life. My entire world. And then, in the blink of an eye, she was gone, taken from me simply because some asshole decided that drinking and driving was the best way to end his night.

Suddenly, our decision to put off having kids was a double-edged sword. On the one hand, raising our kids on my own without Laura there to share in all of their milestones and moments would've been the worst sort of torture. I'm not sure if I would've been able to survive it. On the other, here I was, going through life without her and without a physical representation of our love. Without the ability to watch a baby with her gorgeous smile or the dimple in her chin grow into an amazing human being. Without being able to fully realize and continue the future we'd planned with one another.

At twenty-nine years old, I was forced to adjust and change course. For years, I threw myself into my work because what else did I have to live for? Seth, Melinda,

Benjamin, and even Philip popping up on me, making sure I knew that I wasn't alone was the only thing that kept me from losing myself completely. Well, them and Pepper, the beagle I'd adopted five years after Laura's death.

When I did eventually start dating again, the world had changed, but I hadn't. No one could ever replace Laura, but I didn't want to spend the rest of my life alone either. Hence the string of monogamous relationships I found myself in. Maybe I was chasing something I would never find again, but they were good to me, and I made sure to treat them the same. And while I found myself unattached at the moment—for almost a year now, actually—that didn't mean that a sugar arrangement was what I was looking for, even if it was for just one night.

Exactly why you should just cut your losses and head home.

Now was probably the perfect time to do it. My ever-watchful friends were all preoccupied, Benji and Sage somewhere inquiring about a rope demonstration and Seth and company having found their way to the well-lit end of the bar where, from the looks of it, half the eyes in the place were on them as Alaina fed Melinda candied strawberries. Now was as good a time as any to make my escape. Seth wouldn't even notice—

The thought was only half-finished before I was standing, ready to move out of my dark, slightly hidden corner when someone caught my eye. No, that wasn't quite right. *Something.*

The room may have been dimly lit, but there was just enough light to catch on something shimmering near the entrance. My eyes narrowed a bit, trying to see beyond the glow.

It's a mask, I realized. One that seemed to catch not only my attention but that of a few others in the room as well. And while it was certainly a beautiful sight, it didn't hold a candle to the woman who wore it.

Her black dress stopped mid-thigh, with long sleeves made of sheer fabric. Fabric that skated up each arm, over her shoulders, and everything between her collarbone and the sweetheart neckline of her dress. Despite her petite frame, her caramel legs were long, reminding me of a dancer as she walked gracefully, taking in the sights around her. Her thick, tightly coiled hair looked like a soft crown, framing her heart-shaped face. And even though I still hadn't seen a picture of her and she wasn't wearing the mask we'd talked about, I knew instantly who she was.

Trini.

She was exactly how I imagined her after messaging with her over the last few days and yet so much more at the same time. Even from a distance, it was clear she was nervous.

Funny thing was, I'd finally started to calm down until I laid eyes on her. Suddenly, all of the nerves I'd felt at the beginning of the night were back. Did I wait for her to notice me and come over here, or should I go to her? If I did go over there, did I do it now or wait until she got settled in? If I waited too long, would someone else catch her attention? Yes, we were matched for the night, but that didn't mean she was obligated to stay with me the entire time. Hell, she didn't really have to meet me at all if she didn't want to. That had been made clear in the emails we'd received. You could opt to spend the evening with your generated match or explore your options.

God, I hoped she didn't want to explore her options.

"You're fidgeting. Somehow I thought you'd be too old to be a fidgeter. Guess there are some things you just don't grow out of, huh?"

My eyes snapped open. I had no idea when I'd closed them, but I must have since the woman I'd just spent the last three days thinking about had managed to sneak up on me and we were now face-to-face. Well, as face-to-face as we could be since she only stood at about five foot three to my five-ten. Oh, I'm sorry, five foot three and a half, as she'd stressed to me just the other day. She took that half an inch *very* seriously.

I took her in, at a loss for words.

"And here I thought I'd be the one to make this entire thing awkward. Thanks for taking the pressure off," she said, a small, unsure smile on her face.

I matched it with my own as I chuckled. "You're welcome. I aim to please."

"I sure hope so," another voice said. This one belonged to the woman who must have walked in with Trini, though admittedly, I hadn't noticed her until now. That was a testament to Trini because her friend was certainly hard to miss since we were the same height and she had curves women would die for and men would go to war for. Still...she had nothing on the beauty next to her.

"Khrys..." Trini hissed. Ahhh, so this was the best friend. Interesting.

"Yes, I'm Khrys, and you're Trini, and your friend here is..."

"Arjay," I said, giving her the name Trini knew.

"Oh, good, so I didn't embarrass myself by rambling in front of a total stranger. Excellent."

"Don't worry, I think I'm embarrassing myself enough for the both of us."

"Must be the overachiever in you," she laughed, which in turn pulled one from me.

"Must be. It's nice to officially meet you, Trini."

"Likewise, Arjay."

That smile. Christ, that smile was enough to make my knees go weak, which wasn't an exaggeration. I felt it as my stomach dipped, and I shifted just enough to make sure my legs were still working. They were, but who knew how much longer that would be true.

"Okay, this is cute! Way too cute actually. Look at y'all bantering and what not," Khrys said, breaking the trance her companion seemed to have me in. "It looks like you're in good hands for the night, bestie. On that note..." She turned to me with a serious look on her face. "Take care of my girl, or else we're going to have a problem. Got me?"

I nodded. "Understood."

"Perfect." After whispering something in Trini's ear, she gave me a wave and left the two of us standing there as she made her way to the opposite side of the room.

"Care to share with the class?"

The color rose in Trini's cheeks, something that

managed to make her look both cute and sexy at the same time.

"Ask me again later. If you're lucky, I just might tell you."

"I thought we already covered this, pretty girl. I tend to be very lucky."

CHAPTER FOUR
TRINITY

Arjay was cute.

Wait, no. Cute wasn't the right word for a man like him. Fine as hell was much more accurate, but even that didn't seem like enough. Kind eyes framed by long, dark eyelashes, long locs pulled back and flowing down his back, and a short salt and pepper goatee that complimented his sienna skin just right. How was it possible for someone to be ruggedly handsome and have a baby face all at the same time? I had no idea, but he certainly pulled it off, even in the mask.

Truthfully, I'd noticed him from the moment I entered the room. It was like my eyes were drawn to him, picking up on his energy immediately. I knew it was Arjay even before I'd taken notice of the forest green suit and black button-up he promised to be wearing. He was impossible to look away from. I didn't *want* to look away from him. Shit, I was only vaguely aware of Khrys disappearing because I was so wrapped up in the fact that this man was indeed real and more attractive than I could've

33

ever hoped. If he looked this good with a mask on, he'd probably have my pussy weeping without it.

Like it's not already doing that.

"How about we have a seat?" he asked, gesturing to the dark sofa behind him and snapping me back to reality.

"Sure." I fought the urge to fidget with my mask. It was drawing more attention than I'd originally wanted, but it was too late to switch now.

"I guess you decided to go with Catwoman after all." My face must have shown just how confused I was because he chuckled. "She did have a fondness for sparkly things, didn't she? Seems like the exact type of mask she'd pick out for herself. You just might have more of her femme fatale qualities than you think."

I let out a snort, one that was the furthest thing from attractive, but he didn't seem to mind. "I wouldn't go that far."

"Guess you'll just have to trust me on this one, then."

Before I had a chance to respond, a small bell sounded through the room, capturing everyone's attention. Standing at the very edge of the small landing of the stairs were our hosts, who introduced themselves as Avera and Janelle.

"Hello. Sorry to interrupt, but if you're anything like the two of us, then you're eager to get the evening started. It looks like some of you are well on your way." My eyes followed the same path that the woman who'd introduced herself as Avera's did, landing on a group near the bar doing some interesting things with a bowl of strawberries.

Arjay mumbled something under his breath that sounded suspiciously like, "Christ, not again," but Janelle's voice rang out through the room, drawing my attention back to the front.

"Welcome to A Night with a View. We hope that those of you who aren't as familiar with one another as some of our other guests have had enough time to mingle and become better acquainted with one another."

Avera picked up where she left off in what seemed to be a well-practiced act. "At Sugared and Spiced, our mission revolves around mutual satisfaction. We believe in unique, equal partnerships catered specifically to meet our clients' needs and desires."

"Tonight, those of you who may not be full-fledged members or members at all will get to experience that for yourselves. Tonight, you will find, is all about possibilities."

"About opening yourself up to what could be and indulge in the what-ifs and the maybes."

"Giving in to your impulses and allowing yourself to truly let go because we all deserve the opportunity to explore our desires in a judgment-free zone. That is what makes a masquerade night so perfect."

"We encourage you to wear your masks throughout the night, though you are more than welcome to remove them if you become inclined to do so."

"Share your real names."

"Or don't."

"Gauge your comfort level of interaction, activity, and yes, vulnerability, and then push yourself just a bit over whatever line you've drawn. You may find that it's just what the sugar doctor ordered."

It was Avera's turn to pick up the act again, but I couldn't hear her over the sound of Arjay whispering in my ear. "How long do you think they practiced that introduction?"

"You'll have to be a bit more specific," I whispered back. "Are we talking about the actual speech or the whole call-and-response routine those two have going?"

"Both."

"Oh, they've been practicing that for weeks. Maybe months."

We both snickered, garnering curious looks from a couple not too far from us.

"Now shhh. You're distracting me." I turned back to face the front of the room, which meant I felt more than saw him leaning in even closer.

"Maybe distraction is just what I was going for."

I shivered, even though I was sure my body was warm to the touch. "And maybe I'm too much of a good girl to fall for that."

He chuckled, a sound I wanted to hear multiple times tonight if that was possible. "What if that distraction came in the form of a gift?"

Now that caught my attention. What could he possibly have to give me when we'd just met and only been messaging one another for a few days? I didn't have to wait long before I got my answer in the form of a small wrapped treat.

"You didn't," I whispered, reaching out for it, shocked beyond belief.

"You did say they were your favorite. And I couldn't miss the chance to start the evening off right. What do you think?"

Turning and giving him a small smile over my shoulder, I couldn't help myself when I answered, "I think... you've managed to earn a few points in your favor."

My fingers made quick work of the wrapper, and it was just a matter of seconds before the cherry lollipop was sending sparks along my tastebuds. There was no way in hell I was prepared for whatever this man and tonight had in store for me, but damn it, I couldn't wait to find out.

A TEXT INTERLUDE

ARJAY:

What's the one thing you can't live without?

TRINI:

Oh that's easy. Cherry lollipops.

ARJAY:

I had no idea what you were going to say, but I can tell you it most certainly wasn't that

You sent that back immediately. No hesitation.

TRINI:

Lol no hesitation necessary. They're the quickest way to a girl's heart. Well, this girl at least.

ARJAY:

Why cherry lollipops?

TRINI:

It's just sort of been a weird obsession I've had since I was a kid. They're literally my favorite candy. Upset? They can fix that. Something amazing happened? Great way to celebrate. Bored? Treating yourself to one is a great way to pass the time. Hungry? Perfect snack.

Cherry lollipops are appropriate for any occasion

ARJAY:

I'll have to take your word for it

TRINI:

Don't tell me you've never had one

ARJAY:

I've never been much of a candy person. Scotch, popcorn, and listening to my favorite albums on vinyl are more my speed.

TRINI:

I mean sure, those things sound nice, but I promise you, you're missing out. You haven't lived until you've treated yourself to the sweetness that is a cherry lollipop.

ARJAY:

You'll have to educate me then. Show me for yourself.

TRINI:

...

There you go, getting fresh with me again. I thought you said you would be bad at this.

ARJAY:

Practice makes perfect

But I can stop if you really want me to

TRINI:

Now who said anything about asking you to stop?

ARJAY:

No one 😊

TRINI:

Exactly

ARJAY:

Lol goodnight, pretty girl

TRINI:

Goodnight 😇

CHAPTER FIVE

ARTHUR

I'd miscalculated.

It took all of thirty seconds for it to dawn on me that I'd gone about this all wrong. Did I really expect to be able to concentrate on the introduction and rules for the night after giving Trini that damned lollipop? The answer was yes, but obviously, I was mistaken. What was supposed to be a cute gesture and callback to one of our previous conversations had quickly turned into a silent seduction.

In my defense, I hadn't expected her to unwrap it on the spot. I certainly didn't think I'd be so transfixed on the way her lips wrapped around it that everything our hosts said went in one ear and out the other.

Fuck, fuck, fuck.

As everyone in the room stood, I was at a loss for words but forced myself to follow suit even though I didn't have the damnedest idea what was happening. Was the introduction over already? What had I missed?

Asking wasn't an option because the lollipop was back in Trini's mouth and I was back to being speechless.

Get a damn grip on yourself. You're practically drooling like a college freshman. Are you or are you not a grown ass man?

I plead the fifth.

"You know, I thought a lot about what tonight might look like, but it looks like I underestimated the S&S creativity. This sounds like it's going to be pretty wild. They've thought of everything," Trini said, turning to give me her full attention now that everyone else seemed to be moving on.

"Mhmm, absolutely."

She gave me a strange look before rolling her eyes. "You have no idea what I'm talking about, do you?"

"What makes you say that?" From the smirk on her face, it was obvious that my little act wasn't fooling her one bit.

"Oh, nothing. Well, except the fact that I could practically feel you burning a hole in the side of my face for the last few minutes. Plus you had no reaction to a word Janelle or Avera said, even though I know you were just as curious about what would be happening tonight as I was."

Should I be embarrassed that she'd pulled my card or turned on that she seemed to be so tuned in? Maybe a bit of both. Instead of letting me embarrass myself any more than it seemed I already had, Trini thankfully decided to put me out of my misery.

"You already know tonight's theme is A Night with a View, right?" I nodded because that fact had been included on the email and invitation we'd all received. "Well, that's because they've separated the clubhouse into four different areas, and they all involve some element of voyeurism."

She ticked off each area on her fingers, one by one. "There's The Gallery, where, according to our very enlightened hosts, you can watch Shibari demonstrations and learn something new in a safe environment before you have the opportunity to test it out for yourself. The Hall of Mirrors is area number two, where each of you and your partners' actions and reactions are reflected back to you. Sort of like a funhouse at the carnival, but with sex."

"That's assuming carnival funhouses aren't already seeing their fair share of sex."

A smile played on her lips as she tried not to laugh. "Do you want to know what you missed or not?"

"Sorry, please continue," I said, schooling my features into what barely passed for a serious look.

"Thank you." After clearing her throat in what I assumed was a way to match my playfulness, she started again. "Third is what Janelle called The Studio."

"Let me guess, that's where you can make and star in your own personal films, if you're interested?"

"And watch a few straight-to-video productions if you feel so inclined."

"See, I was paying attention." We both knew that was a lie, but it wasn't hard to figure out what was in store for us there once she'd said the name. Trini was right, though. All of the areas they'd created for the night were definitely interesting. Each had their own merits, and it seemed like no matter where you decided to go, you were in control of how tame or hot and heavy you wanted your experience to be.

"What about area number four?"

"The Viewing Rooms. Apparently, it's another set of rooms similar to The Studio, except instead of videos and screens, they're outfitted with two-way mirrors."

"In case you want to put on a not-so-private show live and in living color."

Trini nodded, causing her thick coils to bounce. Would it be too out of bounds for me to reach out and touch? Honestly, I just wanted to get my hands on some part of her, but the last thing I wanted to do was make her uncomfortable.

Then touching her hair or caressing her cheek like a creep is the last thing you should be doing.

Resolving to keep my hands to myself, I stayed quiet while she picked the conversation back up. "When you really think about it, it's like a mix between the Hall of Mirrors and The Studio, just a little more intimate." Her eyes moved around the room, taking in the other party-goers. "Or people can opt for the fifth option: stay here in the main room, have a few drinks, dance, talk. The lowkey activities, I guess."

"The *non-sexual* activities."

"That too. Something to do for those of us who need a little bit more time to warm up to this whole thing."

Apparently, I had missed quite a bit while I was transfixed on her mouth, which was now just a bit redder thanks to the lollipop in her hand. My focus was where it needed to be now, though, and I caught her subtle use of the phrase "those of us." Trini might be intrigued by tonight's setup, but that didn't mean she was ready to jump in feet first. Hell, I didn't quite feel ready to jump in feet first.

"We could start with a drink if you like. This is all still pretty new to both of us, and I don't know about you, but it's a lot for me to take in all at once. We have all night to explore. What do you think?"

The way her shoulders relaxed told me everything I needed to know, but it was still great to hear her say, "That would be perfect, actually." I don't even think she realized how tense she was until that moment. It made me do a subtle check of my own body language and remind myself to unclench.

"I mean, I do want to go and check things out, but you're right, it is kind of overwhelming."

A small nod from me was all she needed to know that I understood, though I did give myself a mental pat on the back for reading the situation correctly.

My hand instinctively went to the small of her back.

What happened to keeping your hands to yourself?

Instead of dwelling on that thought, I leaned forward. "Is this okay?"

There was no denying the way my stomach clenched as she relaxed into my light hold and gave me a nod. Guiding her toward the bar, it didn't take us long to find a spot since it seemed to have cleared out a bit, the patrons no doubt having gone to see what the other rooms had to offer.

"Just water for me, please." Despite a few of my

nerves returning, I didn't feel the need to order drink number three.

"And for you?" the bartender asked Trini, his body leaning in just a bit too close for my liking.

"A lemon drop, please."

"Sugar-coated rim and all?" She gave him a nod. "Coming right up, sweetness."

He stepped away to make her drink as she scoffed. "You know, it's hard to tell if he's flirting because he thinks I'll actually go for it or because he's looking for an extra tip." Her eyes flicked up to meet mine. "Either way, I'm not interested."

"Noted." It was hard keeping myself in check. The fact that she was going out of her way to assure me that I had nothing to worry about, not that I *was* worried, was sweet. "Are you sure? He's probably closer to your age. I mean, I am twenty years older than you."

"Maybe that's exactly why I'd rather stay right here with you. Guys my age leave a lot to be desired. Seems like it's time I go for a...more mature model. An upgrade if you will."

The words themselves were certainly a boost to my ego, but it was the way she placed the lollipop back in her mouth that was making me weak.

"You're staring again. Is there something on my face or what?"

Shit, how much time had passed? Enough that both my water and her martini had been placed in front of us and the bartender had moved on to flirting with someone at the other end of the bar.

"No, your face is perfect."

The frown she'd begun to sport quickly morphed into a smile. "Does my mask need adjusting?"

"No, not that either."

"Then what is it?"

Why was her genuine confusion so damn cute?

"Truthfully?" My hand rubbed at the back of my neck as I shook my head. "Your lips wrapped around that lollipop is very fucking distracting. And I mean that in the best way possible, though honestly, I don't know if there's a bad way to mean it."

The laugh that she let loose was worth the small bit of embarrassment that I was feeling from my confession. "You sound like a horny little schoolboy right now."

"Trust me, I'm well aware. It's just sending my imagination to some very—ahem—interesting places." I resisted every urge I had to adjust myself, which would only make the whole thing even more awkward.

She nibbled her lip, looking at me through her lashes in a way that seemed to make the world stop. Or maybe it was just the question that followed.

"What if I offered you a taste?"

"Of the lollipop?" The thought of tasting its sweetness just after she had was tempting. More than tempting, honestly. It was downright tantalizing.

"In a way." She took one, then two small steps toward me, bridging what was left of the gap between us. I watched as her hand rose, bringing the lollipop back to her lips and holding it steady as they wrapped around the small sphere. Was this supposed to make things better or worse? I couldn't tell, but damn it to hell was Trini sexy as fuck staring me straight in the eye as she devoured the last traces of the sugary treat.

I swallowed and it sounded so loud, I could've sworn it drowned out every other noise in the bar. "How am I supposed to taste it if there's nothing left?"

"Who says there's none left?"

There was no guessing what she meant then. Not when she was tilting her head back and bringing her hand up to grip the lapel of my suit jacket. In a split second, we'd gone from staring hungrily at each other to pressing our lips together cautiously but curiously. With the slightest amount of pressure, she swiped her tongue over the seam of my lips, silently asking for access that my body demanded I provide. The groan I let out couldn't be helped. Couldn't be stopped. She tasted as sweet as candy and the only thought that crossed my mind was that I *needed* more. Just one kiss and I could already feel myself becoming addicted.

All too soon, she was pulling away, lips slightly swollen and skin heated. "Now I understand why cherry is your favorite flavor," I said as my thumb traced over my mouth, and I wondered just how long it would be before I'd get to kiss her again.

We stood there, grinning at one another for a moment longer before she turned and placed her focus back on the lemon drop. After a few beats passed, I started kicking myself. Was she having regrets? Maybe this was starting to make her uncomfortable. Just as I was parting my lips to apologize, she spoke up.

"I have a confession of my own to make. One that's probably going to ruin the mood because it's not sexy at all. Khrys would actually kill me if she knew I was even thinking of telling you this right now."

My concern had to be written all over my face as the worst scenarios possible ran across my mind. Was this all a giant dare? A joke? Was she married to some big asshole who was going to come barging through the door and attempt to beat my ass just for standing here with her? He could try, but I wasn't going to give up that easily.

A slight chuckle slipped out before I could stop it. "You're making me a little nervous."

"I promise it's nothing scary or overly dramatic. I just... I don't particularly enjoy doing...that."

Whatever *that* was was lost on me at first, but I did my best to put the pieces together. It only took a few seconds for it to dawn on me once I really thought about the timing of her "confession," as she put it.

"Oh. OH!"

Her skin reddened once it was clear I understood what she was saying. "Oral sex has just never seemed fun to me. Like I wouldn't say that I hate it, but it is something I tend to actively avoid." She took a sip of her drink. "Which, trust me, isn't exactly a loss because according to a pretty reliable source, I'm not very good at it anyway."

If Trini sucked dick even half as well as she did her favorite treat, then I was ready to call bullshit on that statement and say fuck whoever let her believe that, but I kept those thoughts to myself. The last thing I wanted to do was give the impression that I was trying to convince her to change her mind. Besides, I was far more interested in the other end of that spectrum right now.

"So giving is a no. What about receiving?"

She shrugged. "I could take it or leave it, really. I mean it's fine, I guess, but I don't really understand all the fuss."

"Maybe you just haven't had the right man on his knees for you."

"Could be." If we kept this up, her skin would be permanently red from blushing all night. I liked the look on her, though. "Are you making an offer?"

The thought of me being that man was almost enough for me to give her a live demonstration. What would she taste like? I was desperate to find out. "If you haven't figured it out by now, pretty girl, I'm sure you will soon."

"Figured what out?"

"That I'd do just about anything for you. All you have to do is ask."

CHAPTER SIX
TRINITY

"You don't even know me."

Arjay couldn't actually mean it when he said I had that much power over him. We barely knew each other. One kiss and a few conversations couldn't be enough to do all that.

The shrug he gave me was so casual, it made his next statement even harder to believe. "I know enough."

Was that something he was supposed to admit? Should I even be worried about whether or not he was serious? We didn't owe each other anything, and technically, for all intents and purposes, whatever happened here didn't have to go beyond tonight. There were plenty of people in this building who were probably just looking for their fun for the night and nothing beyond that. Could I be one of those people? Could Arjay?

From what he'd told me before, that wasn't exactly his style. He also didn't seem like the type of guy to just say what he thought I wanted to hear in hope that it would get him between my legs. Quite honestly, despite my nerves, I didn't think it would take much to let him get a taste of what was between my thighs. I meant it when I said I wasn't exactly pressed over the concept of giving or receiving head, but the confidence in his tone told me that I might want to reconsider my position.

Picking up the martini glass, I threw the rest of the drink back, letting the tart flavor dance on my tongue before swallowing it down.

"Too intense?"

"No," I sputtered, some of the alcohol going down the wrong way. Arjay offered up his water and I took a few sips.

"You can be honest. I won't be offended, promise."

I cleared my throat and got myself together. "No, really, not too intense. Just...unexpectedly honest and earnest. I'm not really sure why it's unexpected, though. It feels like you've been that way in all of the conversations we've had so far."

"Because I have. Lying has never been my forte. It seems pointless when the truth is just a lot simpler."

Narrowing my eyes in suspicion, I asked, "Are you sure you're single?"

He barked out a laugh so loud it got the attention of a few people nearby. "Yes. Positive."

"Just checking."

Somehow, in the last few minutes, Arjay had managed to calm my nerves. My entire body felt relaxed, even though technically we hadn't done anything but talk and flirt a little. Being around him was easy. Dangerously easy, if I was honest, because it made me want to say 'fuck it' and move through the rest of the night without being worried about the consequences. Tonight was about doing something different, and it was time for me to take full advantage of that. No training wheels, no hesitation.

"I think I'm ready to move to another room now."

He gave me a look of genuine surprise. "Really? You're sure?"

"Really." It was now or never, right? Time to channel my inner hot girl.

"Okay." He pushed his glass of water back toward me, and I took that as his way of making sure I finished it. Cute.

I followed his silent request with a smirk playing on my lips before reaching out to take his hand. "How would you feel about The Studio?"

If I didn't think his eyebrows could get any higher, I was clearly wrong. At this point, Arjay looked like a full-on cartoon character as they shot past his mask and almost touched his hairline. The only thing missing was his jaw hitting the floor.

He finally collected himself before asking, "What did you have in mind?"

"Nothing too extreme. Making my film debut isn't on my to-do list today, but watching one could be fun."

Leaving the bar area and leading the way toward a spiral staircase, it was hard not to give myself kudos for ignoring Khrys's insistence that I wear stilettos. Even when she insisted that they were an essential upgrade to my outfit, I knew I didn't need the added pressure of trying to walk around in shoes I'd inevitably stumble in. My black and white Dunks were cute enough for me.

What I did mind, however, was the fact that the narrowness of the stairs meant we had to drop our hands. Using the time to make sure my mask was secure and try not to pout that my excuse to touch him was gone for the moment, we both made quick work of the steps.

"Can you handle another confession?"

The feel of his hand against the small of my back gave me the same warm sensation it had earlier. Were we both looking for excuses to touch one another? God, I hoped so because his touch was doing something to me.

Stomach fluttering? Check.

Nipples hardening? Double check, which was wild in itself because I thought people were just making shit up when they said that happened to them.

A very wet, sticky feeling pooling between my thighs? Ding, ding, ding! We've hit the trifecta, Alex, and quite frankly, I wasn't ready for any of it to go away.

"I'm sure I can. Seems to be one of the things we're good at, after all."

Relaxing into his touch as we hit the top step, I turned so that we were eye to eye. "Adult movies aren't usually my thing. They're definitely not something I've ever watched with anyone else."

There was that look of surprise again. Every time he let it show, it was a boost. Like I was keeping him on his toes. Mark that feeling down in the 'love that for me' column.

"But you want to head to The Studio to watch one?" The confusion in his voice was very clear.

"I don't have a problem with sex work. I mean, it is work, and kudos to the people who decide to do it. But honestly, most porn that I've tried to watch has just seemed...gross to me."

"Gross because...?"

"It just seems exploitative. Like it's solely there to get men off, and quite frankly, the shit that turns y'all on just does not do it for me. And on the off chance I do find a video that doesn't make my stomach turn because the man is doing too much, there's always this voice in the back of my mind that points out that I don't know what the circumstances of the video are, and then I start asking myself a million questions about it, the people, the setting. Everything. It's hard to turn my mind off. So yeah, I tend to stay away from the videos. I prefer my sex scenes in print on my Kindle."

That last sentence pulled a snort out of him, which only made me shrug. I had no shame. Give me a nice smutty romance or erotica scene and baby, watch me work. Or...attempt to, at least.

"Understandable. I'll be honest, I don't think there's any shame in watching adult movies or enjoying them, but they've just never been for me."

"Prefer the real thing?"

"Very much so." The wink he sent me instantly ruined my panties. Oh, wait, they were already ruined. Never mind. "So, what's different about tonight?"

"Well...I appreciated what Janelle said about all of the videos available in The Studio being ethically made." Remembering that he'd apparently spaced out on the entire introduction, I added, "They're all videos that Sugared and Spiced members have made together and decided to share. Sort of like a sugar baby-sponsored OnlyFans."

"Now that's a service I didn't know they offered."

It was genius, honestly. I didn't know if any of the members that showed up tonight had videos on display, but since I didn't know any of them, I figured it wouldn't be awkward.

As we stopped in front of a room with a green light that signaled it was vacant, a thought occurred to me. "Shit, Arjay, you said you have friends who are members. We can go somewhere different, I didn't think—"

A very well-toned arm wrapped around my waist, pulling me in close. My breath caught in my throat, the connection unexpected, but no part of me wanted to pull away. Not even when he leaned forward, pressing his forehead against mine, taking extra care not to disturb either of our facial accessories.

"Take a breath, Trini." Doing exactly as he said was a reflex. I didn't even have to think about it. "Tonight, I don't want you to think about making me overly comfortable. Whatever you want to do, I'm absolutely up for doing, remember? You're in charge here, so if you want to go into this room and watch a woman make a man fall to his knees, then that's what we're going to do. And if that man or woman happens to be someone that I know, we'll laugh about it and choose another video. They can't all be my friends, right?"

Why was it so easy to smile in Arjay's presence? Why was it that a man I'd only talked to for a few days and barely spent more than an hour or two with was able to put me at ease in a way that the man I thought I loved never could?

"A woman." His head tilted to the side, and I let out a breath. "If we go in this room and watch a woman fall to her knees for another woman. I may not watch many movies, but I do know what I like and it tends to be geared toward sapphic videos."

The way his tongue glided across his lips looked tempting enough that I almost leaned in for another taste. Almost.

"Sapphic videos only, then."

I nodded, my confidence coming back for a moment, ready to go into the room, but I stopped again. "There's one more thing." There was no irritation in his eyes, no annoyance in his posture, only curiosity and patience. "I don't...ummm...have the best luck when it comes to self-love."

When his expression only grew more confused, I groaned and pressed my face into his shirt. His arms instantly wrapped back around me, pulling me in close. "I'm just a little bit slow on the uptake, but I'm assuming you mean..."

"Touching myself, yes. Or I guess the adult term is masturbating." Personally, I preferred the former, but whatever.

"As in you don't like doing it? Because I promise you that's not actually what I'm expecting when we go into this room."

"I know. I just wanted to be clear because I know how I get after finding something, or someone, that turns me on. The tingle between my thighs sets in, the hands start wandering, one thing leads to another, and the solo fun begins."

"And if that's what you want to do, you won't hear me complaining."

I snickered. "Shut up." Tilting my head back so that I could see his face, I went on. "Doing it isn't the problem. It's the fact that sometimes, the finished result doesn't actually...happen. Think of it like Russian Roulette. The thrill is always there, but when the trigger is pulled, more often than not, there's nothing to show for it."

Shame wasn't exactly the word I'd use to describe the feeling. More like frustration. Listen, I was all for taking the journey, but when the journey was better than the destination, sometimes it just felt pointless. Add in the fact that my last boyfriend didn't exactly inspire confidence in my technique during partnered activities, and well...

"Your mouth is saying that's not what we're going in here to do, and you may actually believe that. But I just need to know now if you're going to be an asshole about my process if things start going in that direction."

The faint sounds coming from the bar downstairs floated around us as we stood there, staring at one another. And when Arjay finally did open his mouth to speak, it was to say one word. "Okay."

"Okay?" That was it?

"Okay." He nodded. "Since we're being open and honest with one another, jacking off isn't one of my favorite pastimes either. Sometimes it feels unavoidable, but most days I'd rather subject myself to a cold shower. It might sound weird, but touching myself has always felt…I don't know, a little impersonal." For the second time tonight, I wondered if this was something he was supposed to be admitting to me. "So how about we agree that once we enter this room, there are no expectations and no judgments. Let's just see what the night has to offer and, probably for the first time in a while, be kind to ourselves. I don't know about you, but I could use a little of that right now."

Where did Sugared and Spiced find this man? There was no way he was actually real.

"Be kind to ourselves. I think I can manage that."

A TEXT INTERLUDE

TRINI:

So exactly how many of your friends
are S&S members?

ARJAY:

Three, though technically two of them
are members together

TRINI:

Which means what exactly?

ARJAY:

Ha, they're married. They signed up
for S&S last year because she wanted
to look for a sugar baby they could
date together and found one within
like a week. She's perfect for them
actually.

TRINI:

That's...unconventional.

ARJAY:

Maybe in the regular world, but not necessarily for them considering they also started out as a sugar baby couple before they got married.

And did I mention their girlfriend is cousins with my other friend's girlfriend/sugar baby?

TRINI:

Wow. Yeah, you win.

ARJAY:

I didn't realize this was a competition 😂

TRINI:

It's not, but if it was, you'd definitely win. Two points to you.

ARJAY:

Well in that case, I guess you have some catching up to do

TRINI:

Don't get cocky now. I was just starting to like you sir.

ARJAY:

Oh you like me huh? I must be doing something right.

Maybe you should tell me what it is. You know, that way I can make sure I keep doing it.

TRINI:

Honestly? You're just making me think that this whole thing might not actually be a mistake. Making a connection with my preassigned match wasn't actually on my bingo board. I thought it would be more like those school projects you hate participating in, but don't have a choice about because they're 50 percent of your grade.

ARJAY:

That's oddly specific, but relatable.

Is it too corny if I say you're doing the same for me?

TRINI:

Nope. Flattery will get you everywhere.

ARJAY:

Well in that case, pretty girl, please believe me when I say messaging with you over these last few days has been exactly what I needed without me even knowing. I've been looking forward to this all day.

TRINI:

No need to lay it on thick Arjay. I promised to meet you on Saturday and I meant it.

ARJAY:

And I appreciate that, but I mean it. At this point I check my phone so much looking for you that my best friend won't stop hounding me about who the hell I'm talking to. You're causing quite a stir and we haven't even met in person yet.

TRINI:

Awww...are you saying you miss me when I'm gone?

ARJAY:

Maybe. And maybe I'm also saying that game you were talking about earlier? Maybe you're the one that's winning because I'm starting to think you have all the power.

TRINI:

I like the sound of that

ARJAY:

I'm sure you do, pretty girl. I'm sure you do.

CHAPTER SEVEN
ARTHUR

I NEVER REALLY UNDERSTOOD THE PHRASE "THE silence was loud" until this exact moment. The room must've been soundproof because the moment we stepped in and shut the door, it was like we were in our own world.

True to my word, I let Trini take the lead once we entered the well-lit, spacious room. Strings of fairy lights were hung throughout the space, and as she turned in a circle, taking in the scene, each one seemed to catch on her mask and reflect back, creating little rainbows all along the walls. It was amazing how out of everything in this room, the only thing I wanted to focus on was her.

Despite the fact that I might seem cool, calm, and collected on the outside, my nerves were completely on edge. Feeling this off-kilter in Trini's presence wasn't something I'd expected. As someone who prided themselves on keeping a level head, that was proving hard to do right now.

And that kiss...that fucking kiss. It was all I could

seem to think about. Now that I'd gotten a little taste, I wanted more. And while I was willing to wait as long as she needed me to, it wasn't hard to guess that every minute would be torture. I meant what I'd said, though. She was in control of everything that happened, no matter how big or little.

While she made her way over to the large screen on the wall, I finally took the time to notice the rest of the room. Along with what looked like a king-sized bed with red satin sheets, there was a couch that sat along the same wall. Both faced the television, which had two floor-to-ceiling black cabinets on either side.

"If I had this sort of resolution at home, I just might change my stance on videos," Trini said, her voice reflecting the awe that was obvious on her face.

I couldn't help but chuckle. "No, you wouldn't."

"No, I wouldn't, but could you imagine watching *Catwoman* on this thing?"

Yes, actually, I could. With her sitting right beside me in my living room, or in her living room, or maybe while she was splayed out in one of our beds while I knelt in front of her, face planted between her legs. A good movie with a great meal. What more could a person ask for?

"Guess we don't have to wonder where the cameras are."

Her words drew my eyes to the screen, and they widened just a bit at the two figures there mirroring our exact body language. Scanning the room, I finally noticed the cameras that were catching us from multiple angles.

"Production quality is A-1 if I do say so myself."

"You won't hear any arguments from me." Just the

display on the screen suddenly made me wish we both weren't so camera-shy.

Maybe next time.

"See anything you might like?" Just a few strides brought me right behind her. She could see every move I made on the screen since she hadn't changed the channel just yet. Looking straight ahead, I raised my hands, hovering over her shoulders, a silent question hanging between us.

Instead of giving me a nod, her body relaxed into mine, giving me my answer. As my hands pressed down on her shoulders, massaging them slightly, instinct took over and I leaned forward, placing a small kiss just at the edge of her dress.

"Was that okay?" All of a sudden, silent confirmations weren't enough. I needed to hear her say it.

"Only if you promise to give the other side the same treatment." The words were barely out before I was honoring the request, placing a string of kisses along the back of her neck until I reached the other shoulder. "Eager to please?"

"Always." I hope she filed that little piece of information away to use later because every part of me meant it.

Finally clearing the vision of us off the screen, we were replaced by a list of categories. Apparently, in lieu of DVDs, Sugared and Spiced provided the videos using something similar to a streaming app.

"How am I supposed to pick a video if you're going to distract me?" Despite the half-hearted complaint, she continued to scroll through the menu, taking in the stills that were visible in place of actual names.

"You call it a distraction, but what if it's just motivation?"

After getting her to laugh, a sound that got more beautiful every time, I pulled away to give her some space.

"Who told you to stop?" she asked, and the pout she wore as she said it tugged at my heart and the very frustrated member in my pants. Too many of those and I really would give her whatever she wanted.

You're fooling yourself if you didn't think you were already going to do that.

"Don't worry, I'm going to be right here." Standing up the entire time wasn't my idea of comfort, so I planned on taking full advantage of the couch S&S was kind enough to provide. "And you can join me whenever you're ready."

Making myself comfortable, I watched as Trini searched through video after video. The way her brow furrowed told me that she was concentrating. Did everything this woman did have to be so damn cute?

"Found it!" By the excitement in her voice, she was proud of herself. If I didn't know any better, I would've thought she'd found buried treasure. Hell, maybe she had.

"And what is it that you found, pretty girl?"

Strutting over to the couch and taking her seat next to me, Trini used the remote to press play. "You'll see."

There was a moment, just before the movie started, where I worried that she really might have chosen a video starring Melinda and Alaina. This type of entertainment was right up their alley, and it wouldn't surprise me if they'd been more than happy to add to the Sugared and Spiced collection. Thankfully, that wasn't the case. Instead of my beautiful friend and her girlfriend, a very curvy, older, dark-skinned redhead and a slim younger woman with striking pink Bantu knots and a similar complexion appeared, both already in different stages of undress in a room not too different from the one we were sitting in.

"You're so incredibly sexy. Do you know that?"

"You may have mentioned it once or twice."

Their tones were playful, but their movements were anything but. The way they caressed each other's skin, touching just enough to draw attention but not satisfaction. Everything seemed to leave them wanting more, even the kisses they shared.

I cleared my throat, the urge to reach out and touch Trini growing as the women began to moan, but when my eyes glanced over at her, what I saw stopped me.

It was clear Trini was already becoming affected by the display. All the signs were there. From the rise and fall of her chest to the way she pulled her bottom lip between her teeth, there was no denying that she was turned on. Her eyes tracked every movement on the screen. As the beautiful redhead traced the outline of her partner's areola with her tongue, Trini's fingers mimicked the movement on her own breast through her dress. She probably wasn't even aware she was doing it, considering how transfixed she was, but *fuck*.

"Do you see what I see?" I whispered the words in her ear, not wanting to pull her away from the moment but very much needing her to feel my presence.

"That depends on what you see."

My fingers skimmed across the exposed skin of her thigh and she almost turned to look at me. "Aht-aht, pretty girl. Keep your eyes on them, not me."

"But—"

"No buts. You're having such a good time watching them, aren't you?" Moving away from her ear, I trailed my lips along her neck, flicking my tongue against her pulse point. "Aren't you?"

Her yes came out as a gasp, and I couldn't help but smile. "Good. So how about you pay attention to the very beautiful women on the screen, and I'll pay attention to the very pretty girl right in front of me?"

CHAPTER EIGHT

TRINITY

"WHAT WOULD YOU SAY IF I SUGGESTED THAT we get a bit more comfortable?"

Did he expect me to say no to that suggestion? It didn't matter because that two-letter word was nowhere in my mind. My skin felt like it was on fire, and even though the couch was soft, there was a different piece of furniture calling my name. I gave Arjay a quick nod, feeling a surge of disappointment when he leaned away from me, taking his touch with him.

"On the bed."

I did as he said without hesitation, expecting him to climb onto the soft surface with me, but instead, he just leaned back, settling into the couch even more.

"You're not..."

"Oh, I do want to touch you, but first... First, I want to see you touch yourself."

Heat flamed my cheeks. Maybe I should've picked up a full-face mask because I was blushing a hell of a lot tonight. Way more than usual. It wasn't even that wild of a request, but...

"Did you forget what I said earlier?"

"Pretty girl, I remember every single thing you've said and done from the first time you messaged me."

My breath caught in my throat. "Then you know that may not end the way you're hoping it will."

"I don't have any expectations, remember? The only thing I'm hoping for is to get a small taste of the sounds you make when you're making yourself feel good. It doesn't matter to me what that looks like or how far it goes."

Sounded simple enough, but still. "Don't laugh, but that's not something I've ever done with someone watching before."

Maybe Arjay should just become a priest. He'd collected enough confessions from me tonight that I was sure he'd be perfect for the job, considering I'd been so sure he'd be doing most of the talking. Okay, maybe a priest was a bit of an exaggeration. Especially since it would be such a waste for someone as gorgeous as he was, even with half his face a mystery, to swear off women for the rest of his life.

"Never?"

I shook my head.

"Well, lucky me for getting the privilege of being the first. If that's what you want, of course." Those simple words settled my nerves a bit and I nodded, scooting back against the pillow-covered headboard.

"Tell me what you use when you're alone. Pick your poison."

At some point during the introduction, Avera mentioned that each room was equipped with a brand-new set of toys and just about any sexual aid you could think of. Hell, that probably included a few that we didn't. It would be so easy for me to just take my pick. Making this worth Arthur's while, giving him the sort of show I knew he probably wanted despite his words, meant that I should probably choose something exciting, whatever that might be.

On instinct, I stalled while I tried to think of something other than my preferred choice. "I've tried a few different things."

"Yes, but what's your favorite?" He was not going to let me off the hook that easily.

Just tell him.

"My fingers."

There was no other real competition, honestly. Yes, there were toys that could get me there if I concentrated hard enough, but typically I couldn't get out of my head enough to enjoy it when I used them. We could check to see if there was a rose available in the toy pantry, which would make me come, no questions asked, but using that would mean things were over before they even got started. If I was going to enjoy myself, truly enjoy myself, then fucking myself with my fingers was the answer.

"Why?" His question made my nerves rise up again.

"If you want me to use something else…"

"I'm just curious, that's all. No judgment, remember?"

I did, and that made it easy to take a breath and relax myself.

"Because there's something about feeling my fingers sliding across my clit in between fucking into me that just puts me in a different headspace. Like it's not supposed to be there, but it is, and it feels so good I don't want to stop." Even the simple thought of it had me relaxing into the pillows a little more.

"Show me." The command was soft, whispered, but I heard it loud and clear. Watching him intently, I moved to pull down my panties, but his tut stopped me.

"Leave them on. I want you here, laid out in the bed, fully clothed and dripping like you're doing something you have no business doing." His next words came out almost like a growl. "Like you just can't help yourself even though someone could walk in and catch you at any moment."

The forbidden fantasy of the scene he described sent sparks across my skin.

"Eyes forward."

My gaze focused back on the women on screen, barely catching Arjay's movement out of the corner of my eye. What was he doing? Changing positions? Taking off his pants? Leaning forward to watch me intently while he lay horizontally on the couch, back against the arm? My need to know made me desperate, but the need to please him and myself outweighed the desperation so I forced myself not to turn and look. Instead, my eyes took in each movement Bantu Knots made, the way she kissed along her partner's inner thigh. It looked like she was whispering against her skin, but whatever she was saying wasn't picked up by the microphones. There might not be a way to hear her, but how the redhead arched her back in response told me everything I needed to know.

It wasn't long before her face was buried between those thick thighs, and this time, the microphones picked up every single moan that fell from the redhead's lips. I dragged my nails along my covered nipple, thankful that I'd gone braless and grateful for the friction. My eyes fluttered closed at the sensation and I instantly knew I needed more. As I peeked through my lids, I brought my free hand up to my lips and sucked two fingers into my mouth before letting it make its way down my stomach. Within seconds, my hand was dipping beneath lacy material and both fingers were swiping against my slit.

How long had it been since I'd started? My mind couldn't tell if it was a few minutes or an eternity, but it didn't matter. As soon as my middle and pointer fingers pushed past my lips, my swollen clit was right there waiting for any pressure it could get. A hiss filled the room and it was hard to tell where it had come from. Me? The redhead and Bantu Knots? Arjay? Fuck if I knew, nor did I care. No, my singular focus was on stroking that little center of pleasure and twisting my nipple just right and...

"Oh god," I moaned as my eyes snapped shut again. The sound mixed with the moans coming through the speakers but seemed to drown out everything at the same time.

"Again, pretty girl. Let me hear you again," a rough voice called from my right, and at his urging, I swiped again and again and again.

We carried on like that for God knows how long,

with my fingers slipping against my clit and Arjay encouraging me. I was losing track of time. When had Bantu Knots and the redhead switched places? I wasn't sure, but what I did know was that the older woman must've been working magic with her tongue because the high-pitched moans she was eliciting had me envisioning someone else's tongue flicking against my clit.

"Arjay!" His name started as a gasp and ended as a whine.

"Fuck, Trini."

This time I couldn't help myself. I turned my head, needing to know what he was doing to cause the deep grunts coming from his direction, and what I saw made me whimper with need.

He was still fully clothed, just like me, but his hand was wrapped around a very thick shaft as he stroked it over and over again. The tip glistened and, despite what I'd said earlier, the urge to taste his precum hit me like a runaway train.

"Are you wet, pretty girl? Have you ruined those pretty lace panties of yours yet?"

"Mhmm." It was like my fingers had a mind of their own. They'd gone from playing with my clit to dipping inside of my walls, fucking me so good that I had no choice but to arch my back.

"Open those eyes for me." Arjay's command was shaky, like he was barely holding on. "You're having so much fun, but you're missing the show. Don't you want to see the way your girls fuck each other?"

I'd closed my eyes again? When the hell had that happened? Then again, maybe I had been better off not watching because as soon as the screen came into focus, high-pitched whines were pulled from the back of my throat as I bit my bottom lip and fucked myself faster. Redhead was fucking her lover senseless now as she lay flat on her back, and the older woman ground her pussy against hers while pushing the younger woman's leg back, testing her flexibility.

With each roll of her hips, their moans fell faster and louder, and at some point, I realized I might just be outdoing them because damn, did this feel good. Why did it feel so good?

Because he's watching you. Because he's fucking his hand while he watches you fuck yourself and you watch these two beautiful women make each other come.

As if Arjay could read my mind, he said, "You look so damn beautiful playing with your pussy like that, pretty girl. Are you going to come for me?"

"Shit, yes!" The words came out as a groan, and once the truth of them hit me, my eyes snapped to him because I needed to see him. As sexy as what was happening on screen was, it wasn't the sight that I wanted to come to.

My eyes zeroed in on Arjay's hand and the way he thrust into it almost fully in sync with my own fingers, which were back to stroking my clit.

"Good because I'm going to come for you too." His head fell back as his pace picked up and mine followed suit. His hips were lifting on the couch now, and I realized there was only one thing I wanted more than I wanted to come right now.

"Make a mess for me, Arjay. I need to see it."

The guttural groan that followed drowned out every other sound in the room as he did as he was told and hit his release, cum shooting from his dick, covering his hand and shirt, and dripping onto his pants. The sight was enough to send me over the edge, hurtling toward my own peak as I moaned his name again and snapped my legs closed, the sensations almost too much for me.

Blood was pounding through my ears, but I still heard his next words all the same.

"Let me taste it."

They were low and rough, somehow sounding like he was right next to me, yet across the room at the same time. Was that a side effect of my orgasm? My body was still shaking from the aftershocks and it was almost impossible to get my bearings. None of that stopped me from registering his request, though. It was like recognizing some basic, primal need. My hand moved from between my legs, almost on autopilot as I held out my fingers, waiting for him to leave the couch.

He shook his head. "Not like that." Arjay stood, not even bothering to tuck himself away or concerned about the mess he'd made at my request. "Spread it across your lips for me." My heart stuttered. "I'm going to kiss you again, and when I do, I want to taste your cum on both of our tongues."

The whimper that escaped sounded like it came from another person, I barely recognized it. There was a lot of that happening tonight. This man was...nothing like I expected. *Tonight* was nothing like I'd expected.

"Please," he groaned, and just the desperate sound of it was enough to convince me to give in to his request.

Without breaking eye contact, I brought my fingers to my lips, catching the slight glossiness of it in the light. I was using my own essence like it was my favorite shade of lipstick, gliding one finger and then the other carefully and intentionally across my top and bottom lips. His eyes tracked every movement as he came toward me.

It didn't take him long to reach the side of the bed, but Arjay didn't touch me like I'd expected him to. Instead, his hands landed on either side of me as he hovered just out of reach. Taking that as my cue, I tilted my chin up, giving him the perfect angle to have me any way he wanted.

"Where did you come from?"

There was no time for me to answer that question. Not when he was already leaning in. His tongue snaked out, beating his lips to the punch and tracing along the exact same path that my fingers had just taken. It felt like I was barely breathing as I sat there, letting the tip of his tongue move over my lips, tasting my distinct flavor like it was meant just for him.

It must not have been enough because it seemed like a split second before he was kissing me hungrily, like he'd been starving and I was his last meal. The only thing I could do was let him devour me. His teeth nipped me as he sucked on my bottom lip, pulling moans from me that matched his own. And when he slid his tongue into my mouth, tangling it with mine, I squirmed, needing him to touch me because that needy feeling was back, sliding from my gut and down between my thighs.

"I think that kiss tasted sweeter than the first," he said as he pulled away. "Just like sugar."

It was over too soon, and I wasn't ready for that. Not yet, so I dipped my fingers back between my thighs, making them sticky with my cum. "One more taste...just to be sure."

Gripping my hand, his tongue wrapped around my fingers as if they were his favorite lollipop, twirling, gliding, and sliding around them until there was nothing left. And the way he groaned as he did it? Pure filth.

"I don't think I'll ever forget how delicious you are. It'll haunt me in my dreams if I'm not careful."

"Is that your way of saying you're addicted to me already?" I gasped as he sucked my fingers into his mouth.

"You've tasted yourself. Could you really blame me if I said yes?"

"Mmm...no, I don't think I could."

A TEXT INTERLUDE

TRINI:

Have you ever heard of 20 questions?

ARJAY:

Of course I have, lol. I'm not that old.

TRINI:

I just had to check. Okay so what if, instead of 20 questions, we play 20 confessions?

ARJAY:

I don't know...sounds dangerous.

TRINI:

Oh come on, you can trust me. Tell me something you've never told anyone else.

ARJAY:

I give you a confession and then you'll give me one too?

TRINI:

Mmm, I didn't say all that lol

ARJAY:

Maybe I am old because I could've sworn that's how 20 questions worked

TRINI:

Well maybe we're playing by my rules this time

I promise whatever it is will be our little secret

ARJAY:

...

TRINI:

I might be willing to give up one little confession

ARJAY:

Might be?

TRINI:

Maybe. But you won't know unless you take a risk and start us off with yours.

ARJAY:

I think I can do that

I hate watermelon

TRINI:

BE SERIOUS!

ARJAY:

I am lol

I've never actually told anyone else that. All of my friends love it and I've just never seen the appeal.

TRINI:

So do they just never offer it to you?

ARJAY:

They did at one point, but I told them I developed an allergy to it, so I can't have it.

TRINI:

It can't be that serious Arjay. An allergy?!

ARJAY:

It shouldn't be, but telling people I don't like it gets me weird looks and way too many questions. It's just a lot easier to tell people I can't have it as opposed to I don't want it.

TRINI:

Wow

I won't lie, I want to say you not liking watermelon is anti-Black, but saying that also feels anti-Black, so I'll just mind my business lmao

ARJAY:

I appreciate that lol

Your turn

TRINI:

Mmm...I think I need one more from you first

ARJAY:

Haha, of course

You know from my profile that I'm a widower, right?

TRINI:

I remember that

I'm sorry about that btw

ARJAY:

Thank you

So about 5 months after my wife passed away, I got drunk off my ass and did something not so smart.

TRINI:

Not so smart like...

ARJAY:

Like getting married to a complete stranger after going on a two-day bender. The marriage lasted all of 72 hours. We managed to get an annulment and I never mentioned it to anyone ever again.

TRINI:

I mean, that's wild, but why keep it a secret?

ARJAY:

I think because I was ashamed. Not even half a year after losing the woman I loved, I went out and tried to replace her with someone I didn't even know? Not my finest moment.

TRINI:

Maybe not, but you were drunk and grieving. Shit happens. That doesn't mean you were trying to replace her.

ARJAY:

No, but I think on some level, maybe I was. They say drunk minds speak sober thoughts. Maybe my fear of being alone really did drive my decision.

Thankfully, she was understanding since she didn't actually want to be married to me either. I guess we were both trying to heal broken hearts at the time.

TRINI:

Wow

That's not what I was expecting

Thank you for trusting me enough to share

ARJAY:

Thank you for being trustworthy

TRINI:

Well damn. Now I can't give the bullshit confession I was planning to give you.

ARJAY:

I mean you could. Promise I won't hold it against you lol

TRINI:

No, you gave me something real. I want to honor that.

Okay so...

I'm not just in Oakwood visiting my best friend

My mom had a health scare a few months ago. She's fine now, but at the time it really scared her and so she started changing things up like her diet, walking more, taking more vacations with my dad.

ARJAY:

I can relate to that. I did the same after my wife died.

TRINI:

Yeah, well that routine also apparently included admitting to me that my dad isn't actually my dad. He's my stepdad.

ARJAY:

...shit

TRINI:

Lmao yeah that was basically my reaction too

ARJAY:

Did he know?

TRINI:

Yep. They met while she was already like 5 months pregnant with me.

ARJAY:

But you had no clue?

TRINI:

None. I always thought I just took after my mom in the looks department, which I do, but it turns out that there are a few things I do get from my dad, like dimples.

ARJAY:

So you know who he is now?

TRINI:

Yep, he's here in Oakwood. That's why I'm here, to get to know him. He didn't know about me either.

ARJAY:

Wow...how's that going so far?

TRINI:

Not too bad actually. I mean, he's the total opposite of my dad. Well, stepdad. Not in a bad way, just... different.

ARJAY:

I'm sure

At the risk of sounding like I'm stealing your lines, thank you for trusting me with that.

TRINI:

At the risk of sounding like I'm stealing yours, thank you for being trustworthy.

Turns out you're pretty easy to talk to

ARJAY:

You too, pretty girl

You too

CHAPTER NINE

ARTHUR

MY LIPS TRAILED KISSES ALONG TRINI'S JAW and then her throat as she let out a weak moan. After her little demonstration, I'd been more turned on than I could ever remember being and took it upon myself to make her come again with my own fingers. It was clear there wasn't much energy left in her body, not for a third orgasm, but I didn't mind in the slightest. She was gorgeous like this, spent but still vibrating with residual tremors. In fact, it looked like she was beginning to drift off.

With a soft smile, I removed my fingers from her pussy, sucking them clean to freshen up the flavor of her on my tongue, and stood. After a little bit of searching, I found a small aftercare station in the corner of the room and gathered everything I'd need to clean us both up. My shirt and pants were a lost cause, and it hit me that it would make for an interesting conversation when I dropped them off for dry cleaning at my usual place.

Watching the peaceful trace of a smile on Trini's face

kicked me right in the chest and pulled an unexpected request from me.

"You're going to have to repeat that. My brain is still rebooting." The burst of laughter I let out turned that small smile of hers into a full one. "You're laughing and I'm so serious."

"Don't mind me. I was just making one little request."

"Which was..."

"Come home with me."

Her eyes snapped open and watched me as I lay back down next to her. With my weight on my elbow, I cradled my head in one hand while the other traced lazy circles on the inside of her thigh.

"I don't kn—"

"Sorry—"

Our sentences collided together at the same time, causing us both to cut off. It wasn't hard to imagine that we were also probably harboring the same sheepish expression.

"That was presumptuous of me. I'm sorry."

"You don't have to be sorry. I was just going to say I don't know if that's allowed. Would anyone say anything if we just decided to leave together?"

"I can't imagine why they would. The only people who may have something to say about the whole thing would be our friends, and if my first impression of Khrys is correct, she'd probably be celebrating right along with the group of heathens I spend time with." Trini let out a snort at that, most likely because she knew I was right. Or maybe it was my use of the word 'heathen.' "The whole point of tonight was to make connections, right?"

"Right."

Silence overtook the room as she contemplated my proposal. Or maybe she was thinking of a nice way to turn me down. Going home with an older guy she barely knew? I knew I wasn't dangerous, but if she was being cautious, I couldn't fault her. But the urge to have her in my bed was so strong it practically had me by the throat.

"Or we really could stay here. It's okay. We can forget I asked. I'm happy to spend time with you wherever you want to do that. Assuming you do want to keep spending time with me, that is."

"Why?"

Confusion twisted my features. "Why?"

"Why would I want to stay here when I could be in your bed right now, letting you have your way with me?" There was heat in her eyes, and it took everything in me to suppress the growl building in my chest.

"Well then, why indeed."

She let loose a giggle. "Let's go."

"You're sure?" It may have been annoying, but I needed to be sure she was doing this because she wanted to, not because she felt like she had to.

"I'm very sure. Just like I'm also very clear on the fact that your emphasis on consent is sickeningly sexy." Now it was my turn to chuckle. "There will be more kisses and orgasms, right?"

"Pretty girl, please hear me when I say the only thing I want more than one of your kisses right now is to have you in my bed, legs spread and pushed back as I fuck into you over and over again."

"Well, how is a girl supposed to turn that down?" She leaned up to give me one of those kisses that I'd come to crave so much.

"Let's get out of here."

I stood first before helping her out of the bed. The video she'd chosen had ended without either one of us noticing, causing the screen to default back to the Sugared and Spiced logo. There were two thoughts running through my mind as we made our way back downstairs toward the host stand.

"Leaving so soon?"

Instead of the man who had checked me in when we'd arrived, Janelle and Avera were standing there with knowing smirks on their lips. Despite a few hours having passed since I'd gotten there, it was clear that most of the attendees were still enjoying what the two hosts had to offer.

"Yes. That's not a problem, is it?" Trini asked.

"Of course not. As long as you're both leaving together of your own free will, you are more than welcome to take your fun elsewhere," said Avera. Her eyes took in our appearance, and I was sure she knew exactly why Trini's dress looked askew and no doubt what the stain on my dark pants was as well.

"And we hope to see you back soon to have even more fun with us," Janelle added with a wink.

I moved to take off my mask. "Thank you."

"Oh, you can keep that if you like. It may come in handy later."

Maybe, but if we were going back to my house, I wanted Trini to know exactly who she was going home with.

"And I appreciate that, but I think I'd rather leave it here."

Something in my tone must have hinted at the hidden meaning behind my words because Trini moved to take hers off as well. "Agreed."

She made quick work of the ribbon and slid the mask from her face, revealing the fact that she was just as beautiful as I'd imagined her. No, even more so. Only, unlike when I'd turned over my mask, Avera refused to take hers.

"Absolutely not. That mask is too stunning for you to give back. We insist that you keep it."

Trini didn't need much convincing. "Well, if you insist..."

"We do," confirmed Janelle. "Just let the valet know which vehicle is yours and he'll bring it to you quickly. I'm sure you're both very eager to have a bit more privacy."

Eager wasn't even the word for it. After saying a quick thank you, I placed my hand against Trini's lower back and we made our way out of the front door. True to our host's word, the valet was there waiting and scanned my invitation's QR code just as he'd done when I'd arrived in order to identify my vehicle. While we waited for him to return, I used my grip on her to turn her body toward mine.

"You are...fucking gorgeous, pretty girl."

She smirked as she placed her hands on my chest and

allowed me to lean in to steal another kiss. "And you are very, very handsome, Arjay. It's actually unfair how fine you are."

"Arthur." Her eyebrows rose with interest. "My real name is Arthur. I wanted you to know that before we left." I leaned in again, this time to whisper into her ear. "Just so you know exactly which name you'll be moaning very soon."

Whether it was my words or the feel of my breath on her skin, I couldn't be sure, but I took note of the shiver that ran through her.

"In that case, Arthur, I'm Trinity. And I'm happy to say that it's very, very nice to meet you."

CHAPTER TEN
TRINITY

Like everything else tonight, the time it took for us to leave the clubhouse and arrive at Arjay— I mean Arthur's front door seemed to be a contradiction. Somehow, it took forever to get there, yet it wasn't nearly enough time for me to get ready for what I knew was coming next.

"I should have mentioned something on the way here," he said, pausing in the middle of unlocking the door.

"Uh oh..."

"No, it's nothing serious...I hope. It's just that I don't exactly live alone."

Wait a minute.

I didn't have to wonder for long what he meant because the moment we walked through the door, my eyes landed on a white and chocolate beagle laying right in the middle of the foyer.

"That's her favorite spot to lay and wait for me to get home," Arthur explained sheepishly.

"She's adorable!" Moving past him to get to the real star of the show, I dropped down and scratched her behind her ears. "What's her name?"

"Pepper. This is really her house. I just pay the bills."

I giggled as she gave a low bark, probably in agreement, before licking my hand and trotting off to the left.

"Goodnight to you, too!" he called after her. "Now that I'm home, she'll want nothing to do with me until she needs something, which probably won't be until some ungodly hour in the morning."

"Love that for her."

With the lady of the house gone, it was just the two of us again. The nervous energy was back, full force and flowing through me, putting me on edge. I'd barely been able to handle it when Arthur wasn't touching me. What the hell was I going to do when he was finally inside of me? All that big bad shit I was talking before we left was slowly trickling away now as he gave me a quick tour of the house and let me wash my hands in the hallway bathroom.

"So, what do you think?" By the sound of his voice and the way he rubbed the back of his neck with the hand that wasn't holding mine as we made our way toward his bedroom, I wasn't the only one feeling the nervous energy.

"Very nice. Definitely not the bachelor pad that I was picturing," I teased.

He chuckled, easing the tension that seemed to have built between us. "I'm well past the age of having a bachelor pad."

"Good to know." As I said the words, we stopped in

front of his door. With one more look in my direction, he led me inside and took a small step back, letting me take everything in. By the time my eyes found their way back to Arthur, the nerves were fighting to come back. It must have been written on my face.

"We don't have to do anything that you don't want to do here. You know that, right?" He paused, as if to give me time to process his words, but I'd heard and understood him loud and clear. After a beat, he took a step closer, coming out of the doorway. I swear the closer he came, the louder my heart seemed to beat in my ears.

Once we were close enough to touch, a question fell from my lips before I could stop it. "You changed your mind?"

Arthur just laughed. "Absolutely not. Far from it. Trust me when I say I'm here with you because I very much want something—anything—to happen. You are..." The way his eyes traveled over me felt like a caress, and my god, did it feel good.

"I am...?" He couldn't just start a sentence like that and not finish. Not when that wet, sticky feeling was back between my thighs. Hell, maybe it had never really left.

"Magnificent."

Yep. One word and the floodgates were very much open. The man was talented. I just wondered how far that talent went and what else he'd be able to do.

"But just because I haven't changed my mind doesn't mean that you can't. This whole thing is still new for both of us, and if anyone knows how difficult it can be to step out of your comfort zone, well, it's me."

"I think that ship has sailed, don't you?" What we'd done in The Studio was well past both of our comfort zones and yet felt natural all at once.

"We've certainly had some fun tonight." The mask that had been hiding my face for most of the night was in his hands. As he tossed it on the nightstand, he turned his gaze back to me. "But that doesn't mean you're ready to take this to the next level. And I don't know, maybe I'm going a bit overboard here, but..." His words trailed off, but instead of saying anything, I just let him collect the rest of his thoughts.

"It's just important to me that you know you don't owe me anything, no matter what we have or haven't already done. I want you to feel comfortable with me, no matter what. I want to feel you in every way possible, but I'd be just as satisfied sitting here with you, watching a movie and digging into the other bag of lollipops I bought, if that's what you want."

He was giving me an out. One that I could take and he wouldn't be upset or pout or throw a tantrum about it like some men might. I might not have known Arthur for long, but I felt confident with that assumption. And even though reiterating my right to consent to this whole thing was the absolute bare minimum, it didn't stop his words from hitting me both in the chest and between my legs.

Screw the nerves. I wanted this. "As delicious as cherry lollipops are, I don't know whether or not I should be insulted that you think they would be half as satisfying as fucking me."

"Now when on earth did I say that?"

That was it. That was all he said before he was on me in a flash. Between one breath and the next, as he gripped the back of my neck, he gave me his first request.

"Can I undress you?" Arthur's words caressed my lips, sending a wave of need through me. All it took was a simple nod before he was stepping behind me, brushing my thick curls to the side carefully with one hand while the other slowly pulled down the zipper of my dress. The small piece of metal dipped all the way down my lower back to the top of my ass, landing right in the middle of a small but intricate set of red, yellow, and orange wings.

"What do we have here?" I could hear Arthur shifting, gripping my waist, and the image of him getting on his knees for me was mind-blowing.

My eyes closed as I arched slightly. That spot had always been sensitive, but his fingers added more electricity than usual.

"I'm sure at your age, you've heard of tattoos."

There was that chuckle of his again. "I have. I'm quite familiar with them."

That caught my attention, making me turn my head just enough to gaze down at his face. "Don't tell me you have one?"

"Six, actually."

"*Six?*" That was a shock.

He nodded, clearly amused by my reaction. "Not as strait-laced as you thought, huh?"

"Apparently not." Though would a strait-laced man spend his Saturday night covering his hand in his own cum while watching me get myself off to two beautiful women? It was hard to say. "Seems like we're both full of surprises."

My mind reeled, trying to picture where his body art might be.

"Don't worry. You'll find out soon enough." There he went, reading my mind again. "These are wings?"

"Phoenix wings."

"Favorite animal?"

"You do know that phoenixes aren't real, right?"

"Doesn't mean they can't be your favorite." *Touché.*

"Well, in that case, no. That honor goes to the giant panda." I turned back around and faced the bed again.

"Ahhh, that explains the shoes sitting by my front door, then." A giggle slipped out before I could stop it. "So, why phoenix wings?" The second time he let his finger move over the tattoo pulled the same reaction out of me as the first.

"For the same cliché reason most people get them, I guess. Freedom and new beginnings."

I thought for sure he'd ask why I'd placed them there instead of someplace like my shoulder blades, but instead, Arthur did something that sent a different sort of shock through me. Just like the zipper had done a few moments before, his tongue followed a path along my spine all the way down to the topic of discussion. There was no stopping my whimpers.

"Doesn't taste like a cliché to me," he groaned against my skin.

He spent the next few seconds pulling down my dress until it pooled on the floor around my feet. I sent a silent thanks to Khrys, wherever she was, for convincing me to pop the tag on the pair of black satin thongs buried at the bottom of my underwear drawer. That, and her words of wisdom to go without a bra.

As his eyes roved over me, caressing every inch, I asked, "You're not going to do that thing men tend to do where I'm the one who spends most of my time out of my clothes while you stay fully dressed, are you?"

His eyes glittered with amusement. "Well, the thought had crossed my mind to get down on my knees for you, right here, right now, in this very expensive suit." The image his words invoked in my mind made me realize that I would give anything to see that. "But...I wouldn't want to deprive you if what you really want to see is something else."

His hands gripped my shoulders, guiding me until the back of my thighs hit his bed and I had no choice but to take a seat. "So tell me, pretty girl, how do *you* want *me*?"

It was actually out of this world how sexy he could make two simple words like 'pretty' and 'girl' sound when he put them together, let alone used them in a sentence like that one. My eyes tracked every movement as he began to unbutton the top of his shirt.

"Don't get quiet now. Use your words."

My teeth gripped my bottom lip as I eased myself back toward the middle of the bed. "I want to see you." The words came out just above a whisper, but I knew he'd heard them. "I want to see everything."

He didn't need another word from me. His fingers moved deftly over the buttons, undoing them one by one until the shirt was open, exposing every bit of his chest, stomach, and the happy little trail underneath.

Well, that answers the question of where at least two tattoos are, I thought as I took in the bear tattooed on the left side of his chest and the cross against his right ribs. It was hard to stop myself from licking my lips as I wondered what his skin tasted like. The thought was so distracting, I almost missed it as he dropped his pants and briefs in one move, baring himself to me. Hmmm... tattoo number three looked like a tribute of some sort that wrapped around his left leg.

There wasn't much time to focus on it, though, nor did I want to once my eyes traveled a little higher up. That beautiful dick of his had been on display in The Studio, but looking at Arthur now, when no part of him was hidden away, trumped the filthy sight from earlier tenfold.

"It's my turn to taste you."

The surprise was written all over his face. "But I thought..."

"I know what I said earlier and it very much still stands...outside of this room. Outside of you. At least for right now." He reached down and stroked himself a few times, precum beading up at the tip, and a small smile played on my lips. "Now, would you please come here? You're wasting it."

"And we can't have that, can we?"

I shook my head while he stalked closer to me and readjusted until I was on my knees at the edge of the bed. This wasn't the first time I'd ever given head, but it was definitely my first time being excited about doing it.

When he was standing right in front of me, my hand reached out to grab his shaft almost like it had a mind of its own, pulling a groan from him as he let go. Without looking up, I knew Arthur was on the verge of saying something. Whatever it was, I didn't want to hear it. Right now, I was only interested in one thing.

If I thought the groan he let out just from me touching him was something, it was nothing compared to the sound he made or the way he nearly tipped over as I took him into my mouth. The slightly salty flavor sitting on the tip of his dick caused me to let out a moan of my own as I lapped at it, needing more.

"What if I told you," I started as I pulled away just enough to get some air, "that the way you taste comes very close to replacing my favorite flavor?"

Dipping my neck, I took him back into my mouth and hummed around his shaft. With my eyes closed, there was no way to see what Arthur looked like, but I felt him the moment his hand gripped the back of my head.

"Fuck." Every groan he let out was motivation for me to go harder. I gave him a rough stroke and opened up wider, letting his dick slide further into my mouth until I gagged for just a moment. I'd always thought gagging while giving head was the least sexy thing in the world, but the way my pussy tingled at the reflex proved me wrong. Arthur must have agreed because his grip grew tighter, trying to hold me in place. I wasn't quite ready to give up control just yet, though.

My head bobbed back and forth, perfectly timed with the rough strokes of my hand. Each time he hit the back of my throat, a string of curses left his mouth, and my eyes fluttered shut as I moaned. Was there anything I wanted more right now than him fucking my throat? No, and that admission felt wild to me, but my entire body was on fire. My pussy was wetter than ever, slick and needy, and the thrill of it all was heady.

A pull on my scalp yanked me back and I whimpered, actually whimpered. Not because of the pain but because that salty treat was back and I wanted more. "Arjay," I whined, leaning in again.

"The way you're moaning around my dick is driving me up the wall, pretty girl. I need to be inside of you. Now."

I scrambled back eagerly because one thing for sure, I didn't need to be told twice.

CHAPTER ELEVEN
ARTHUR

AFTER A PERFORMANCE LIKE THE ONE TRINITY had just given, I wasn't sure if I was being held up by my own strength of will or if the bed was doing all the hard work. Or maybe it was just my need to be inside of her that was driving me to hold myself upright, hovering over one of the most beautiful women I'd ever seen. Let's be honest, it was the last one, which was why I was also smiling at her like she was the first bit of sunshine after a stormy day.

I groaned as her hands glided over me, coating my thick shaft with lubricant. The need to check in with her one more time took over. "Are you sure this is what you want?"

"I promise you, Arjay—Arthur—I wouldn't be here, naked and open in your bed, gripping your very impressive dick if this wasn't what I really wanted." I felt her fingers skim along my chest, sending shivers down my spine.

As I notched myself at her entrance, my other hand

caressed her cheek. "Just doing my due diligence to check in, pretty girl. I want to take care of you."

"And I love that for me. Consent is sexy and you absolutely have mine. Right now, though, what I need is for you to fuck me." My heart beat against my chest at her words, like it was trying to burst right out of my ribcage. "You wanted to taste me and now *I* want to feel *you*. I *need* to feel you."

Her tongue peeked out, tracing along those delectable lips of hers. "Are you going to give me what I need, Arjay? Or do you want me to beg for it?"

My hips gave a small, almost involuntary thrust at her words. Did she know how much it turned me on when she talked like that? If not, it was time she learned that lesson.

"Open up then, pretty girl. Let me in."

With my hands gripping on each of her legs, I pushed them up and a little further apart, folding her into the perfect position, her knees toward her chest. The lube did its job just a little too well, causing me to slide halfway into her with just one thrust. An almost pained grunt escaped me, accompanied by her own gasp as Trinity arched her back. This angle, what the hell was I thinking fucking her at this angle?

My head dropped forward and she immediately cradled it in her hands, allowing me to press my face into the crook of her neck. Christ, I wasn't even all the way in yet and I was already putty in her goddamn hands. Literally.

"It's so thick," she whined, and I could feel her hips trying to move under me, but thanks to this position, she wouldn't be able to move until I let her. Not with my weight on her the way it was, but if the moan she let out was any indication, she didn't seem to mind.

"I know. Fuck, Trinity, I know, just...just give me a second." My heart was beating too fast and my dick gave a slight pulse. If I wasn't careful, this was going to be over long before it actually started, and how embarrassing would that shit be?

The sound of Trinity gasping my name when I finally collected myself enough to pull up and roll my hips to press the rest of the way into her was one of the best things I'd ever heard in my life. What in the hell was this? A mistake? Had I made a mistake? Some part of my brain was telling me I damn well had because how the fuck was I ever supposed to let her go after knowing how she felt wrapped around me, warm and wet and pulsing and...

"Goddamn!" I barked out, thrusting again as she angled her hips up and I bottomed out. My teeth clenched. "You're not playing fair, pretty girl. Not at all."

She let out a giggle as her hands found their way to my waist. "You're kidding, right?"

Another roll of my hips was the only way I could show her that I was not, in fact, kidding. Trinity gasped, back arching again, offering up those perfect breasts of hers as a treat. What sort of man would I be if I didn't indulge? At least, that's the question I asked myself as I leaned forward and flicked my tongue along her already pebbled nipple before sucking it ever so slightly.

Her next words were something between a whine and a moan. "You're the one not playing fair." And yet, instead of pushing me away, she swirled her hips and buried her fingers into my hair to keep me exactly where I was.

"Would you like me to stop?" I asked when she finally let me up for air, though no part of me was complaining.

"Don't you fucking dare." Her hands moved to my backside, gripping my ass like she was afraid I might do exactly what I suggested.

"Mmm, I don't know." My strokes stuttered, slowing down from the steady pace I'd begun to set. "Maybe that's exactly what I should—"

"Arthur, pleeease." Damn, did I love hearing my real name on her lips. It sounded like heaven, but then, was that really any sort of surprise when her pussy felt the exact same way?

One of her fingers slipped down, finding its way to my puckered entrance. The sudden shock of it drove me forward and forced my eyes closed. When they finally reopened, my gaze snagged on the cheeky grin on her lips.

"Playing a bit dirty, aren't we?"

"You have your games. I have mine." The twinkle in her eye was just as contagious as her smile.

"Well, then..."

There were no other words as I leaned back, straightening my posture. If she wanted me to fuck her, then that was exactly what I was going to do. Each stroke felt like it pressed me deeper and deeper inside of her. Like I was touching every part of her. Or maybe it was the other way around. Maybe Trinity was the one touching every part of me. I felt her everywhere, not just wrapped around my shaft, though the heat of her was absolutely making her presence known there. Each one of my senses seemed to be connected to her.

The taste of her skin on my tongue, slightly salty, but unlike anything I'd ever had before.

The feel of her pussy clenching around me, sucking me in and refusing to let me go.

The sound of her moaning my name, her pitch climbing higher and higher with every breath.

The sight of her, arms above her head as her eyelids fluttered closed and her hands grabbed for something, anything, to hold onto.

The smell of her perfume, just a hint of cherry in the air, enveloping me in a way that made me want to give her a lifetime supply of whatever the fragrance was just so I could smell it whenever I wanted.

Five senses, one woman, the combination knocking me right on my ass.

"I'm so close." The words were just a whisper, but I heard them loud and clear.

"Tell me what you need."

"I don't..." Her words trailed off and I slowed down my thrusts, ending each one with an extra roll to help her get there.

"Yes, you do. Tell me." Heat began to lick its way up my spine and I knew it wouldn't be long before I went over that cliff. I needed Trinity to get there first almost as much as I needed air to breathe. Hell, maybe even more. "Use your words, pretty girl."

"Pressure!" The words came on the end of a stroke that made even my toes curl. Using her hands to show me exactly where she wanted the pressure applied, she skimmed her fingers along the skin of her stomach. "Right here."

Quickly, without hesitation or thought beyond giving her exactly what she needed, I covered Trinity's hand with my own. Careful not to press down too much, I leaned forward, letting a fraction of my weight do the job for me.

She gasped. "More."

Another lean. A moan this time. Christ, did I love that sound. "*Pleeease!*" Mmmm, I think I loved it even better when she begged. "Harder!"

Was she asking me to fuck her harder or press down more? It didn't matter. I gave her both, losing track of how many strokes I was actually delivering or how hard my hand was pressing down at this point.

"I feel it. *Ooooh, shit!*" She let out on a high-pitched wail as her walls clenched around me.

"Come on my dick, pretty girl," I growled. "Be a good girl and do what you're told."

"Make me." There was a challenge in her voice, fire in her eyes. "If you think you can."

Think? Oh no, no, no. I *knew* I could. Unleashing the last bit of strength I had, I pounded into her, so much force behind each thrust she moved along the bed, almost hanging over the edge. And just as that familiar feeling made its way from my toes, all the way up my body, Trinity began to shout her release. I waited as long as I could to pull out, until I knew she was satisfied. The world began to go black at the edges, leaving me just enough awareness to lean forward and capture her swollen lips with my own in one of her intoxicating kisses as my cum painted her stomach.

Despite the fact that we were both clearly spent, we kissed each other hungrily like we couldn't get enough. Then again, at this point, I was sure I would never get enough of Trinity.

Finally pulling away to give us both some much-needed air, I collapsed next to her. There was no way I would be able to get my legs to work well enough to the bathroom to get something to clean her up with. Even lying here, I could tell they felt like Jello. So instead, I leaned over the edge of the bed, grabbing my shirt, and used that to wipe my release off of her skin.

"Now why would you do that?" Trinity pouted. "I think I liked being branded by you."

This fucking woman. "I'll try and remember that for next time." Because if it were up to me, there would undoubtedly be a next time.

Silence fell over the room, even our breathing barely making a sound, though both of our chests were heaving. I had no idea how much time had passed when she broke it. "Did you know?"

My brain was still trying to catch up to my surroundings. Had I ever blacked out like that before while coming? Shit, not that I could remember. It was clear she was asking me a question, but I couldn't focus enough to understand the actual words.

When everything had finally settled down and her question registered, I found my voice. "Did I know what?"

"That it would be like that."

My face turned and our eyes met. The shyness was back, so different from the woman who'd just been begging for me to make her come on my dick. So different and yet very much the same because both versions of her had me under their spell. "No. I had no idea. If I had, I might have prepared just a bit better."

That pulled a laugh from her as she cuddled in close, fingers splayed across my stomach as I wrapped an arm around her. "If you'd been any more prepared, I don't think either one of us would've survived."

"Hell, I'm not sure I did." There was another pause before I asked, "You never did tell me what Khrys said to you earlier."

She yawned as I kissed the top of her forehead. "Oh, nothing. Just that if I was a real friend, I'd wrap your locs around my hand and hold on for dear life before the night was over."

I nearly choked hearing that, which sent her into a fit of sleepy giggles. "I'm not sure how much pulling you did tonight, but the night's not over just yet. There's still time."

When no response came, I peeked down. Just that fast, Trinity had fallen asleep. Maybe I really had died and gone to heaven because nothing had felt this perfect in a very, very long time. And in the morning, I'd make sure she followed up on Khrys's request because it sounded like a damn good one to me.

A TEXT INTERLUDE

ARTHUR:

I think you were right

TRINITY:

I keep telling Khrys that I usually am. What should I tell her I'm right about this time?

ARTHUR:

I do already miss you when you're gone

TRINITY:

Arjay, it's only been a few hours

Maybe 4 hours tops

ARTHUR:

Doesn't make it any less true

Come back

TRINITY:

Honestly, I would if I could. Especially after that little sendoff you gave me 😌. Probably the best goodbye I've ever had.

ARTHUR:

Well I do aim to please, remember?

And that wasn't goodbye. That was 'see you later'. As in, 'see you in a few hours because I don't think I can stand to be away from you so let me give you something that will make you miss me as much as I'll miss you'

TRINITY:

You said all of that to my pussy this morning?

ARTHUR:

Sure did. She didn't give you the memo? If she can't follow instructions then you might really need to come back so I can teach her a lesson.

TRINITY:

OMG you are ridiculous 😂

ARTHUR:

Maybe, but that's neither here nor there

So are you on your way? You know it'll be worth it.

TRINITY:

Oh, I know it would be.

But I promised my dad that I would meet him for lunch and thanks to your very long message this morning and Khrys's very nosy questions, I'm already late.

ARTHUR:

😖

Fine, I'll just sit here and suffer all alone.

TRINITY:

Not these dramatics sir

ARTHUR:

Lol

Seriously, enjoy lunch with your dad. Spending time with you is a gift so he better appreciate it. Or he and I are going to have a problem.

TRINITY:

Is that so?

ARTHUR:

It is

TRINITY:

...

I'll be over once we finish. Give me two hours.

ARTHUR:

Take your time, pretty girl. I'll wait for you as long as you need me to.

TRINITY:

Promise?

ARTHUR:

Promise.

CHAPTER TWELVE
ARTHUR

THE MOMENT TRINITY LEFT MY BED, I WANTED her back in it. It was unexplainable the way I craved her, even after such a short time. It'd been a week since our first night together, and despite the fact that we both had to go on living our regular lives, that hadn't stopped us from spending night after night together, and mornings too. If it were up to me, she would be right next to me while I whispered every nasty thought that ran through my mind whenever I looked at her. Instead, here I was alone, nursing a beer because my pretty girl already had plans with her father.

As much as I wanted to pout about it, I didn't. She'd been spending quite a bit of time with him this week, which was what she came to Oakwood to do in the first place. And I was happy for her. From what she told me while we watched *Catwoman* for the fifth time in the past week, he was an...interesting man.

"But we do the same snort and laugh combination."

"Oh, do you? I'm sure it's a lot cuter when you do it."

"Oh, it is. But he laughs at all of my really bad jokes, so he gets extra points for that."

It took everything in me not to ask if I'd get a chance to meet him before she headed back to see her mother in a week. And to go along with that question were the ones about if I'd get to meet her mother and when she'd be back, but I kept them all locked in my head instead of asking them aloud. The last thing she needed was a grown ass man clinging to her when she had other things going on in her life, especially considering how new this all was. Trinity was under enough pressure without me adding to it. We didn't owe each other anything, and despite what I wanted, even I realized it was too soon to be asking any of those questions.

Shaking the thoughts from my head, I made my way over to the group as they gathered around Philip, who was acting like he was holding court, as usual. At least with the focus on him, I wouldn't have to endure more nagging questions about where I'd disappeared to on masquerade night and every night this week. Whatever it was that he had to tell us, though, I wished he would get on with it. Listening to the man blow smoke up his own ass was painful, even if we were friends.

"So what's this grand announcement you've gotten us all together for, Philip?" Benji asked, taking a sip of his beer.

"And for the love of God, don't let it be another hotel." That grumble came from Seth, putting a smirk on my lips.

Philip gave them both pointed looks. "If I recall

correctly, neither of you were complaining about that hotel when you needed rooms to have your fun in."

Well, he had them there. Actually, maybe I should look into asking Philip for a suite tomorrow. Trinity would probably love the spa, and the thought of her riding me on soft hotel sheets and ordering room service after was a very appealing one.

"Yes, and you never let them forget it, you pompous ass." Sage's voice came behind us as she walked up, arm in arm with Alaina. The rest of us snickered, including Philip, who grinned at her wolfishly. It was no secret that she still wasn't his biggest fan. Did she like him more or less than she did a year ago? Honestly, it was hard to tell.

"And I probably never will," he shot back. *Less.* Guaranteed she liked him less. "But no, this isn't about another hotel or even about the one I already have. There's another new development in my life. One I didn't see coming but am excelling in, like most of life's challenges."

Forget smoke, this was a whole forest fire. We all looked at each other, confusion and interest plain on our faces. There was no way he got us all together to announce he was getting married...was there? This was a man who rarely slept with the same woman twice as far as I knew. If anyone were to ask me what Philip's mortal enemy was, the first thing that would come out of my mouth was *commitment*. It was clear I wasn't the only one who'd been thinking the same thing.

"Don't tell me you're getting married. Not after all that shit you gave me about asking Sage to move in." Was Benji trying to make Sage hate our friend?

"Who is she because she needs to know she might be making the worst mistake of her life." That came from Melinda, but I couldn't say I disagreed.

"Hell no. That's a lane I'm more than satisfied with letting the rest of you live in. No, this is a different kind of commitment. One none of you have ventured into yet, so it's understandable that you didn't immediately think of it. It's uncharted territory."

"Please just get on with it," I sighed. If we hurried this along, I might just be able to convince Trinity to meet me downtown for dinner before we went back to my place.

"So impatient. I'm talking about fatherhood."

I choked—actually choked on my drink. It was so bad Seth damn near killed me as he hit my back in an attempt to help.

"Philip, I mean this in the nicest way possible. Who the hell let you get them pregnant?" Alaina laughed in disbelief.

"That would be my mom, apparently," a voice said behind us. A very...very familiar voice.

It can't be.

Philip's eyes lit up in a way that I don't think any of us had ever seen before as he gazed at its owner, and the only thing I could do was say a silent prayer that I was wrong about my assumption. That the voice didn't belong to who I thought it did—the woman whose naked body had been the center of my world for the last seven days.

And of course, whoever was supposed to be listening didn't actually give a shit because as we all turned, my eyes collided with that exact person. The last person I'd expected to see was also the very person who seemed to be the cause of my best friend's happiness.

"Everyone, I'd like you to meet my daughter, Trinity."

A TEXT INTERLUDE

ARTHUR:

This may very well be the most
awkward thing I've ever experienced

Please tell me this is a joke

TRINITY:

This is LITERALLY the least funny
thing that's ever happened to me so,
no, it's not a joke.

ARTHUR:

Did you know?

TRINITY:

What? That apparently all of my long-
lost father's friends belong to a sugar
baby organization and it was going to
lead to me having mind-blowing sex
with one of them right under his nose?

Yeah, of course I knew

ARTHUR:

What happened to this being the least funny thing you've ever experienced?

TRINITY:

I decided to test it out and see if maybe I was wrong

What do you think? Is it actually hilarious?

ARTHUR:

...

Maybe just a bit

TRINITY:

Maybe a lot a bit considering that smile on your face

ARTHUR:

Are you staring at me?

TRINITY:

Nope, just taking a little peek. You're the one who's been staring for the last hour.

ARTHUR:

Is it my fault that you showed up here looking like a fucking five-course meal?

Even when I need to be on my best behavior, I can't keep my eyes off you, pretty girl.

There's no point in asking me to try

Don't tell me you're blushing. Fuck, that makes you look even more beautiful.

TRINITY:

Oh my god, stop!

ARTHUR:

Can't help myself. Who knew I'd be here, just minding my business and torturing myself thinking about not being able to see you all day, only for you to show up, ready to be served up to me on a silver platter?

TRINITY:

Arjay...

ARTHUR:

And then you have the nerve to be sucking on that lollipop like that? I think you want me hard and desperate for you. Is that what you want, pretty girl?

TRINITY:

Maybe...

ARTHUR:

Or maybe you want to treat me to one of your sweet, addictive kisses. You know I can't get enough of your lips.

TRINITY:

Remember when you told me how horrible at flirting you were?

You lied

ARTHUR:

Is it really flirting if I'm just telling the truth?

TRINITY:

Yes

Meet me in the basement bathroom in 7 minutes?

ARTHUR:

What about daddy dearest?

TRINITY:

We'll deal with that later

Right now, there's only one daddy I'm concerned about.

A FINAL WORD

Thank you for reading Sugar-Coated Kisses. Arthur and Trinity may have put me through it, but I love the end product and I hope you do. Don't worry, you'll see more of them and their story in the final installment of the Sugared & Spiced series, which stars Philip getting his just desserts in more ways than one.

Until then, if you're able, please find the time to leave a rating and/or review on your favorite platform (Amazon, Goodreads, Storygraph, etc.). They're the best way to help readers find new favorites and so important when supporting indie authors.

To keep up to date on upcoming Lady Marie projects, be sure to sign up for the Spice In Your Life Newsletter and follow me on social media @ladymariewrites. To order a signed copy of any of my paperback projects, merch, or web exclusives, please visit the Lady Marie Shop at www. ladymariewrites.com

ACKNOWLEDGMENTS

You all already know I have a team behind me that is unmatched. People who are in my corner no matter what and are always there when I need them. They know who they are. But I really want to thank the readers. Y'all truly keep me going even when I'm not sure that I can. You're supportive, patient, and believe in me even when I don't believe in myself. The way y'all eat these stories up is amazing and I'll never be able to thank y'all enough. As long as you've got me, I've got you.

ALSO BY LADY MARIE

SISTERS & SERENDIPITY SERIES

Worth It (A Fake Dating Novel)

Found Forever (An Established Couple, After the HEA Novella)

SUGARED AND SPICED SERIES

Sugar, Sugar (An Age Gap, Sugar Arrangement Novella)

Sweet Heat (A FFM Age Gap, Sugar Arrangement Novella)

Sugar-Coated Kisses (An Age Gap Insta-love Novella)

Sweet Control (An Age Gap, Sugar Arrangement Novella)

SLEIGH THE NIGHT COLLECTION

After Tonight (A Brother's Best Friend Novella, *Sleigh the Night* Prequel)

Sleigh the Night (A Winter Shorts Collection)

HOLIDAY NOVELLAS AND SHORT STORIES

With Sugar on Top (A Sugared and Spiced NYE Short)

Sinnamon & Golds (A Lick Back Season, Thanksgiving Novella)

Szn's Greetings (A Sinnamon & Golds Christmas Short)

Resolutions (A New Year's Novellette)